Book 2 in th

MW00982078

Camp Liverwurst
& the stray compass

Jim Badke

Camp Liverwurst & The Stray Compass
by Jim Badke
©2023, James Badke
ISBN 978-1-7777101-5-6

Cover & Author Illustrations: Mike Fehr
Cover Design: Jennifer Bush (www.northernedge.co)

Author Page & Blog: www.jimbadke.ca
Purchasing, Articles & More: www.campleader.ca

Also available from Amazon in Kindle eBook format, readable on any device with the free Kindle app.

Contact Jim (www.campleader.ca) for bulk orders or if your organization is interested in translating this book.

Related books by this author, available on Amazon:
- *Camp Liverwurst & the Search for Bigfoot* (2022)
- *The Christian Camp Leader* (2013)

A Note to Cabin Leaders:

This series of middle-school novels is designed to be read aloud to your campers over the course of a week at camp. Every 10-minute chapter can be used to spark conversations about God. Questions and activities are provided at the end of the book to be used as prompts (not a script!) for discussion. Plan on reading two to three chapters per day—for cabin devotions, during wake-up, after a meal or on a break. Campers will likely ask you to read more each day!

WHAT LEADERS ARE SAYING ABOUT CAMP LIVERWURST:

"In this mysterious fantasy, Jim crafts a wonderfully imaginative story, helping the reader see the Gospel through the eyes of a camper who is wrestling with difficult questions about God. What a fun story! And what a great read for a counselor with young campers at camp, to help open up meaningful conversations!" – Pat Petkau, ED, Forest Springs Camp & Conference Centre, WI, USA

"Jim has provided an innovative, tangible and creative way to facilitate the important relationship between a camper and their cabin leader, and a camper and God. An excellent resource for cabin leaders to encourage God discussions." – Sharon Fraess, National Director, Christian Camping International - Canada

"Fun. Imaginative. Original. Jim Badke's Camp Liverwurst *brings the world of Bible camp to life in a most unexpected way. Complete with discussion questions, this book will engage your campers' minds and hearts with a story that is sure to create thought-provoking discussions on what it means to be a follower of Jesus."* – Bill McCaskell, National Director, One Hope Canada

"A captivating and fun-filled adventure. Cabin leaders love using the story to present biblical truths. Campers can't get enough!" – Chris Burdge, Executive Director, Camp Imadene

"I look forward to reading this book to my campers, who will be eager to see what the next chapter holds. A great way to spark conversations about Jesus!" – Janelle Ten Have, Cabin Leader

--- More reviews at Amazon.com ---

Also in this series by Jim Badke:

Camp Liverwurst & the Search for Bigfoot

Jayden is best at worrying.

When his friend Evan invites him to summer camp, Jayden freaks out. He never expected a boatful of wild animals. Or out-of-this-world camp leaders. Or being good at almost everything. Or a real, live Sasquatch in the woods. But unexpected help is on the way!

Camp Liverwurst & the Search for Bigfoot is Book 1 in the new *Camp Liverwurst* series of short read-aloud novels for middle-school kids about camp.

Cabin leaders, teachers & parents love reading chapters to their kids to spark conversations about Jesus.

Included are questions and activities to prompt Bible discussions about faith in God and overcoming fear.

ISBN 978-1-7777101-2-5

CONTENTS

1. The Beautiful Accident

On the second-to-last day of school, Maddie was hit by an avalanche. It wasn't snow or rocks or anything interesting. Just every textbook, gym shoe and old lunch bag in her locker, cascading down on her head before crashing to the floor.

A few students laughed as they walked by. Maddie was furious as she gathered up her stuff. When a boy kicked her hand sanitizer down the hallway, she grabbed her math book and threw it at him as hard as she could. He jumped when it smacked another locker just past his head. "Oo-ooo!" said everyone in the hallway, staring.

"Maddie! What on Earth…?" Maddie's homeroom teacher came out of her classroom just in time to see the book hit the locker. "I think you and I better have a talk." She helped Maddie put her things in the locker and waited for her to enter the classroom. They sat by the window and watched streams of students leave for their rides home.

Maddie didn't know what to say. The worst part was that this teacher was her favorite. She hated the disappointed look on her teacher's face. "I'm sorry, Ms. Williams," she murmured, almost too quietly to hear.

"Let me guess," her teacher offered. "Some boy likes you, and the way he decides to show it is to steal your combination and stack your locker." Maddie looked surprised. Her teacher laughed. "I remember! It happened to me too, years ago. At least that's what we called it: 'stacking a locker.' Is it still called that?"

Maddie shook her head and angrily wiped away the tears she couldn't hold back. "It's just being mean! I don't care if he likes me." She laughed through her tears. "At Christmas time, he put a tree in my locker, with decorations and everything." Ms. Williams handed her a tissue. "I've never even talked to him. I wish he would leave me alone."

"Do you want me to speak with him?" Ms. Williams asked.

"No! I mean, I can handle this myself, thanks." Maddie tossed the tissue at the garbage can but missed. "It's almost summer. Maybe the guy will go to another school next year. Or get hit by a falling piano."

Ms. Williams looked shocked and then sighed. "Maddie, what's going on with you? What happened to the happy, thoughtful girl I started the school year with? And where did this angry, explosive one come from?"

Maddie looked down and didn't answer. Not out loud, anyway. Inside, she too wondered what had changed in the past year. Everyone was upset with Maddie. Friends avoided her. Sydney, her little sister, stood up and left any room Maddie entered. Maddie always got along well with her parents. Not anymore.

Ms. Williams watched the dark look on Maddie's face with concern. "Maddie," she said quietly, "tell me about one thing you're looking forward to."

Maddie gave a half-smile. "Well, normally I would say my week of summer camp. But I'm not sure if I'm even excited about that anymore." She sighed. "Everything seems so…"

"Pointless?" Ms. Williams suggested.

"I guess," Maddie answered. "I was going to say 'stupid,' but I didn't know what you would think of me. Like, I should be grateful I can go to camp every summer, right?"

"Tell me about your camp." Ms. Williams sounded interested.

Maddie's smile grew a bit. "It's been my favorite spot forever. One of my friends always says there's no place like it on Earth. The camp is beside a big lake up in the mountains, and you can only get to it by boat…"

"You don't mean Camp Liverwurst, do you?" exclaimed Ms. Williams.

"You've heard of Camp Liverwurst?" Maddie was astonished.

"Heard of it? I went there every summer when I was a kid!" Ms. Williams laughed. "Did you ever have Abigail as your cabin leader? Or Rahab?"

"You gotta be kidding! I love Abigail! But I don't know Rahab." Maddie's bad mood faded as she remembered. "What about Noah's crazy animals?"

"And David and Meriam's music!" Ms. Williams' eyes danced.

"And archery tag!"

"Martha's chocolate chip cookies!"

"Skookum the Sasquatch!"

"Wide games with Queen Esther!"

Together they shouted, "Fresh huckleberry ice cream!" and they gazed at one other, laughing. They could see in each other's eyes that they both knew about Camp Liverwurst.

"It doesn't sound like you think Camp Liverwurst is 'stupid.' " Ms. Williams observed.

Maddie's smile faded. "I love going to camp, but I think that might be part of my problem."

"Please help me understand, Maddie." Ms. Williams gave Maddie her full attention.

Maddie closed her eyes and thought about what to say. "Well, I was hiking with my dad a while back, and we watched this gorgeous sunset. And my dad said, 'The world is an incredibly beautiful accident.' " She looked up at her teacher. "I guess he meant that everything we see in the world happened by chance, right?"

"Yes, that's what many people believe," said Ms. Williams. "But you've heard this idea all your life."

"Yeah, I guess so. But it never hit me before as it did then, watching the sunset with my dad. Like, I'm a part of this world! Which means I'm an accident too," Maddie finished sadly.

Ms. Williams also looked sad. "If you're an accident, Maddie, you're also a very beautiful one. But what does this have to do with Camp Liverwurst?"

"Well, you know," Maddie answered. "The people at camp talk about God all the time. But if God made everything, my dad is wrong about the universe happening by chance, right?"

"So you feel caught between two worlds," said Ms. Williams. "Is that it? One world with a Maker and one without?"

"That's just how I feel! Like it's a tug-a-war, and I'm the rope," Maddie agreed. "I love my parents and I love the people at camp, but it's hard to do both at the same time. I don't know who I am anymore," Maddie sighed. "And I guess that's why I'm grumpy all the time."

"Well, I do hope you decide to go to Camp Liverwurst this summer, Maddie." Ms. Williams smiled at her. "When I was a camper, I first figured out who I was when I understood who Jesus is. I hope the same for you." They stood, and Ms. Williams returned Maddie's hug. As they walked out of the classroom, she added, "In the meantime, Maddie, will you promise not to teach any more textbooks how to fly?" Maddie laughed and nodded.

A week after school ended, Maddie was still unsure if she wanted to go back to camp or not. If she gave her spot to someone else, what would the leaders at camp think? They would assume she was being kind and generous. Would anyone miss her? Was going to camp worth all the confusion it caused her? She had almost decided to tell her mom and dad that she didn't want to go. Then she received a text from one of her best friends:

Olivia: Hey Maddie you all packed up for camp?

Maddie: Nope. Haven't even started

Olivia: ??? whaaaat??!! Why not?

Maddie: I haven't decided if I'm going

Olivia: Yikes Maddie!!! Don't move I'll be there in 10 minutes

Olivia was at Maddie's door in five. Maddie gave her the "don't talk" signal because her parents were in the kitchen. Neither said a word until Maddie closed her bedroom door. "Well?" asked Olivia, eyes wide as she sat on Maddie's bed. "What's the deal, Maddie? I thought you were the last person who would ever miss a week of camp!"

Maddie stared at her friend for a moment. "Olivia, do you ever wonder if what they teach us at camp is true? I mean, about God and stuff?"

"I don't know," answered Olivia. "I guess I don't think about it a lot." Her eyes lit up. "Like, we searched for a real, live Sasquatch last summer! Who gets to do that?"

"For sure, camp is fun. And the leaders are… well, you know. Out of this world!" Maddie sighed. "But what they believe and what my family believes are miles apart. Like, how can I go to camp and sing songs about God when my dad thinks there's no such thing as God?"

"Maddie, what I think is that you think too much. You can do both, you know! Be a Jesus girl at camp, and when you get home, switch back to being… I don't know, Earth girl." Maddie bit her lip and looked troubled. Olivia continued, "Besides, I know for sure you're going to camp this summer."

"Why?" exclaimed Maddie. "What do you mean?"

"I mean, remember Evan telling us this is his last summer at camp?"

"So what?" Maddie tossed her head with a frown.

"So, I know you've liked Evan for-EV-ver!" Maddie pushed her right off the bed, but Olivia didn't stop. "As if you'll miss your last chance to hang out with Ev-aaan for a week!"

"Olivia, not so loud!" Maddie warned her friend, looking at the door but unable to keep the smile off her face.

"Well," teased Olivia, "what do you think?"

Maddie pulled Olivia up off the floor. "I think that going to a camp because of a boy is a terrible idea!" And then she laughed, "I love it! Okay, I'll go!"

The closer it was to her week of camp, the more excited Maddie became. Not because of Evan—he was just a bonus—but because she loved camp. And maybe Olivia was right. She might be overthinking the whole God thing. Maybe it was okay to live in both worlds, with and without him. Who said she had to be only one person? Maddie could be whoever Maddie wanted to be, whenever and wherever she wanted.

The night before camp, Maddie had another text from Olivia:

Olivia: I'm so pumped for camp I keep squealing out loud mom can't wait for me to leave

Maddie: Who do you think our cabin leaders will be?

Olivia: IDK but I hope it's Abigail again

Maddie: Yeah but it would be fun to get to know someone new

Olivia: What do you mean new they're all ancient remember

Maddie: ROFL

Olivia: See you in the morning Maddie

Maddie: See you in the morning

2. An Unexpected Crossing

When Maddie and Olivia arrived at the Camp Liverwurst parking lot, the first person she saw was a bald man with a big beard. He was riding—she could hardly believe her eyes—a unicorn. It was the most beautiful creature Maddie had ever seen. "Noah!" Maddie gasped. Olivia stood beside her with her jaw dropping and bags falling to the ground around her feet. "Where on Earth did you find that?"

"Hey, Maddie, Olivia! Welcome back!" Noah dismounted and led the unicorn toward them. It snorted and shied, but Noah patiently and gently held the reins. Olivia looked like she was about to faint. Noah handed the reins to Maddie. "Well, I didn't exactly find it on Earth, at least not in your time period. Getting a couple of unicorns to camp this week required permission and some spacetime travel. Handsome beast, isn't it?"

Maddie reached out and gently placed her hand on the unicorn's snowy forelock. The animal nuzzled up to her, resting its horn lightly on her shoulder. She could feel its quiet, powerful breath. After a few moments, the unicorn's breathing slowed and the horn became heavier. "Uh, Noah," Maddie murmured nervously, "what is it doing?"

"Ah, unicorns are known to grow sleepy in the presence of young women," Noah explained. Maddie staggered under the weight of the drowsing creature. Noah slapped its flank, and the animal slowly lifted its heavy head. "Looks like you have a new friend, Maddie!"

Maddie was about to ask Noah the unicorn's name, what he fed it, if she could ride it and a million other questions. Then she felt a hand on her shoulder and heard an unfamiliar voice. "Maddie? I've been looking all over for you. Your whole cabin group is at the boat and ready to leave." Maddie turned to face a woman with long, dark hair and a healthy glow. The unicorn snorted and pulled on the reins. Flustered, Maddie burst out, "Excuse me! I don't think I know you!" It was not a good beginning.

Noah stepped forward and took the reins from Maddie. "Let me introduce you. Maddie, this is Rahab, and she will be your cabin leader this week. It's been a while since she last came to Camp Liverwurst, which is why you haven't met before." Maddie had no reason to glare at her new cabin leader, but she glared anyway. Noah turned to Olivia. "And you're back with Abigail this time, Olivia. I saw her loosening her mainsail cover a few minutes ago. You know where her boat is, right?"

Now Maddie's jaw dropped. "What?" she shouted. "Olivia and I aren't even in the same cabin? What is this?" The unicorn shied nervously. Noah was about to reply when Maddie continued angrily, "You know, I almost didn't come this summer! Now I wish I hadn't!"

In the sudden silence, Maddie saw several faces in the parking lot turned in their direction. She had made a scene again. Noah spoke quietly. "No one will make you stay against your will, Maddie. This is your choice. Either way, we love you, which means we want the best for you."

An angry reply came immediately to Maddie's mind, but she forced it down. She glanced at her friend Olivia, who looked like she was ready to cry. She glared again at the stern, impatient face of her new cabin leader. Maddie turned to Noah and looked longingly at the unicorn. How had things gone from her best dream come true to her worst nightmare in only a few moments?

She said flatly, "Fine. I'll stay." Already, she imagined ditching Rahab's cabin group all day and only sleeping there at night. And no one would stop her from getting a ride on that unicorn. She gave Olivia a hug, grabbed her bags and marched off after Rahab toward the dock.

Camp Liverwurst is situated across a long, deep lake surrounded by snowy mountains. The only way to get to the camp is by water, and cabin groups might make the trip on any kind of boat. As Maddie approached the lake, she saw Noah's ferry with the usual giraffes and pandas and every other kind of animal looking over the rails. All along the dock, she saw canoes and kayaks, paddle boards and windsurfers. She passed Abigail's sailing yacht, which she knew so well and where Olivia was already aboard. Everywhere, campers and leaders stowed their gear and made ready to disembark.

Rahab led Maddie to a small boat she had never seen before. It was long and narrow and pointed at both ends. Her new cabin group was busy stuffing their bags under the five wooden planks that served as seats. The boat had no mast, and Maddie didn't see a motor. Only a pile of long oars on the dock.

"Hey girls," Rahab called, "this is Maddie! Let's help her find space for her stuff." Maddie recognized a few of the girls, but none had been in her cabin in previous summers. Two of them took her bags and jammed them under a seat at one end of the boat.

One girl stepped out of the boat and introduced herself. "Hey, Maddie! I'm Ava. Is this your first time at Camp Liverwurst?"

Maddie shook her head. "No, I've been…"

But she didn't get to finish her sentence. Rahab was handing each camper an oar and shouting, "Time to go, girls! Everybody in. My boat is pretty wobbly, so no standing! Sit down right away." She bustled the remaining girls into their seats and took her place at the back.

The other cabin leader sat at the front, facing the campers. "Okay, everyone!" she called out, "if you haven't met me yet, I'm Priscilla, and I will be your assistant cabin leader." She had curly hair and was warm and cheerful. "Before we go, you need to know the two sides of the boat. Does anyone remember what this side is called?" She pointed to her right, where

Maddie was sitting. "Port!" Maddie shouted. She knew it from sailing with Abigail.

"That's correct! Your name is Maddie, isn't it? I'm glad you're on board with us." She looked at the other girls. "And this side?" She pointed to her left.

Since no one was answering, Maddie shouted, "Starboard!" She pronounced it **star**-*bird*.

"Right!" smiled Priscilla. "Maddie, you must be a sailor." Maddie nodded. "So," Priscilla continued, "since I'm facing the opposite direction, is port on my left and starboard on my right?"

Maddie knew this. "No, port is always on this side, no matter which way you're facing. When you're facing forward, port is on your left. I just remember that 'port' and 'left' both have four letters."

"Thanks, Maddie!" Priscilla laughed. "That's helpful. And here's why it's so important. Where are my starboard rowers?" The girls glanced at one another. Eventually, the ones on the starboard side raised their hands. "And my port rowers?" Their hands went up right away.

"Perfect!" continued Priscilla. "Now, as we are rowing, I will call out the commands. It's important for our safety that you listen and follow them right away. And it's even trickier because you won't be able to see me. Know why?" The girls shook their heads. "Because you're all facing the wrong way! Rowers always face the back of the boat, which is called…"

"The stern!" Maddie shouted.

"Yes, and my end is called the 'bow.' Everyone turn around!" There was a chaos of bodies and paddles as the campers all tried to swivel at the same time.

"Stay seated!" Rahab shouted sternly as some tried to stand and the boat rocked under them. Now they were all sitting and facing her, which Maddie didn't like. In fact, she liked Rahab less and less.

"Great! Now we're ready to go!" Priscilla's voice came from behind them. "Your first command is to 'Ship Oars!' No, it doesn't mean to toss your oar overboard, Lizzy." The girl leaned over to retrieve her oar. "It means to hold your oar straight up and down between your knees, with the flat part up and the handle end resting on the bottom of the boat." After some near collisions, ten oars were pointing up. Maddie noticed that the boat had drifted away from the dock.

"You're an excellent crew!" exclaimed Priscilla. "Now we're going to 'Ship Oars Out.' Slowly lower your oar so it rests on the side of the boat between the two pegs next to you. Maddie, do you know what the pegs are called?" Maddie did not. "They're called 'thole pins.' Maybe we can thing them thumb thole muthic!" Only Maddie laughed.

In the next few minutes, the girls learned enough commands to make their heads spin. Easy On Port. Hard On Starboard. Let Her Run. Hold Water. Ready All, Row! Soon, they were rowing across the water.

The whole time, Rahab steered with another oar that was set between thole pins on the pointed stern. Occasionally, she called out a command of her own, which Priscilla repeated. But mostly she seemed to watch each girl as they rowed. When she was watching Maddie, Maddie scowled back at her.

Rowing was hard work. They got into a rhythm as Priscilla called out, "And, Stroke! And, Stroke!" to keep the girls all pulling their oars at the same time. They were soon working up a sweat. You would think that with so many rowers, it would be easy. True, they were moving pretty quickly through the water. But pulling on the oars seemed harder every time Priscilla called out the stroke. Whenever Maddie glanced over her shoulder, the other side of the lake looked just as far away. And Rahab just sat there, steering.

3. The Terrible Cabin Leader

It was a sunny and beautiful day. The lake was calm, with tiny ripples in patterns all around them. The boat glided swiftly and left a small wake behind it. By the time they reached the middle of the lake, Maddie was so warm that she wanted to dunk her head over the side. Priscilla seemed to read her mind. "Let Her Run! Ship Oars!" The boat coasted for a distance before slowing to a stop. "Anyone feel like taking a dip?"

"But we don't have our swimsuits on!" one girl protested.

"Is that stopping you, Chloe?" Priscilla laughed. "C'mon, kick off your sandals and hop in! Oh, and make sure there's nothing important in your pockets." Chloe shrugged, pulled off her sandals and stood up—then remembered not to and sat down again. "It's okay, Chloe," Priscilla reassured her. "You can stand in a second." She turned to the girl who shared the plank seat with Chloe. "You get ready too, Rylie. You'll both jump in at the same time." When both girls were standing on their seat, trying to keep their balance, Priscilla said, "One, two, three, jump!"

Soon, all the girls were splashing around in the lake. At first, Maddie was freaked out about swimming in the middle of a huge, deep body of water. But since they still had their life vests on, there was nothing to worry about. Maddie lay back, watching two small clouds race each other across the sky. The cool water felt wonderful after rowing in the sizzling sun.

Then she felt something nibbling at her toes.

Maddie shrieked and pulled her feet away, thrashing in the water. She heard two girls laughing. Rylie and a camper whose name she couldn't remember were floating where her feet had been. "Oh Maddie," laughed Rylie. "You were hilarious! I wish I'd caught that on my phone."

Usually, Maddie would have laughed too. But she didn't know these girls, and was already angry about being in their cabin group and not in Abigail's with Olivia. She kicked hard with her feet, splashing the two girls and moving away from them. She heard Rylie yell, "Hey, stop that! Can't you take a joke?" But Maddie didn't care. She avoided a circle of girls who were hitting a beach ball to one another. Instead, she swam by herself until it was time to get back in the boat.

When Rylie glanced back at Maddie, she didn't look angry. She looked hurt. Maddie felt a twinge of guilt about how she had reacted. But it was time to row again, and Maddie scrambled to follow Priscilla's commands. Rowing with wet clothes was cooler but not comfortable. Maddie's arms hurt, and she felt like she was getting a blister on her thumb. She wished again that she was sailing with Abigail and Olivia without a care in the world.

After what felt like another ten thousand strokes with her oar, Maddie heard voices and laughter. She turned and saw they were approaching the dock in front of Camp Liverwurst. Unfortunately, turning around made her lose her stroke and clash oars with the girls behind and in front of her. She mumbled a "Sorry!" Behind her, Ava said, "It's okay, Maddie! All of us have done that. You're a pretty good rower if it's the first time you bumped oars with someone." Maddie wanted to turn and smile at her, but was afraid she would mess up again. Besides, Priscilla's commands were coming thick and fast now: "Woah, Hold Water! Easy On Port. Starboard, Ship Oars. Port, Let Her Run. Port, Ship Oars. And now everyone stay put until we tie up to the dock." Minutes later, the port rowers were handing luggage up to the starboard rowers.

They had arrived at Camp Liverwurst, Maddie's favorite place ever. But all she could think about was how much she wanted to be anywhere else.

As Maddie followed the other girls along the dock, a boys' cabin group was walking down the gangplank of Noah's ferry. Every animal you could imagine accompanied them, including two snowy unicorns, each with a boy on its back. Maddie's heart screamed with envy. One boy waved and yelled, "Hey, Maddie!" Her heart did a flip. It was Evan, and the other boy was his friend Jayden.

Maddie dropped her bags and ran to the boys and their unicorns. When Maddie reached them, she was careful not to come too close to the unicorns. She didn't want them to fall asleep under Evan and Jayden! "Wow, I'm glad to see you guys!" Maddie exclaimed. "So far, my day has been…"

But she was interrupted. "Maddie, stay with your cabin group," she heard Rahab call. "We're going to our cabin now. Keep up, please!"

"Who's that?" said Evan.

Maddie's smile disappeared. "Her name's Rahab, and she's a terrible cabin leader." In her heart, Maddie knew her words weren't fair, but her all-too-familiar rage was growing again. "I guess I gotta go," she said dejectedly. "See you around, okay?" She patted the unicorn on the nose and ran off to catch up with the other girls.

Maddie was in no rush to reach her cabin. By the time she arrived, all the girls had gathered around the building. "There's no door!" she heard Ava say. Sure enough. There was a sign that said "Jericho," but the cabin had only windows high up, and no door.

"Look, over here!" Lizzy called from the side of the cabin. "It's a kind of ladder." Everyone ran to Lizzy and saw a bright red ladder from the ground to the top of the window. But it was a ladder made of rope!

"Is that how we get inside?" asked Rylie excitedly.

"Yes, it's the only way in," Rahab replied. "It's my preferred method. A rope ladder keeps out unwanted visitors. And it's a way of coming and going without being noticed," she continued mysteriously.

But the rope ladder was tricky to climb. Thankfully, there was a separate rope to haul up their bags. But even without bags, climbing the ladder was like trying to climb a wriggling snake. When Maddie tried, the ladder spun around and she bashed into the side of the cabin. No one could make it up very far.

Rahab and Priscilla watched without offering help. When Lizzy got herself impossibly tangled in the ladder, Rahab unraveled her and set her on the ground. "Watch!" she said. The girls gasped as Rahab ran up the ladder like a spider.

"Your turn, Maddie!" Rahab called down.

"I can't do it!" Maddie shouted. "You saw me—it's hopeless!"

"I have high hopes for you, Maddie!" Rahab replied calmly. "Come, start with your right foot on the bottom rung. No, not in the middle; all the way to the right. Now, reach up with your left hand and grab the rung above your head. Do you feel balanced? Good!"

Maddie discovered that she didn't swing around this time. Rahab continued her instructions. "Okay, in a moment, you're going to step up to the next rung with your left foot. At the same time, grab the rung above your head with your right hand. You must transfer all your weight from one hand and foot to the other at the same time. Ready? Go!"

It was so easy. Maddie stepped up with her left and grabbed with her right. It seemed natural to keep going, right and left, left and right. The girls cheered her on as if they were chasing her up the ladder. She was soon able to swing herself through the open window into the cabin.

Rahab gave her a double high-five. "Well done, Maddie! I was sure you could do it. Now it's your turn to help the next girl make it up."

Soon, all the girls and their luggage were inside. The cabin was full of voices and laughter as they picked their bunks and set up their beds. Maddie was thinking about how good it felt to be the first girl to make it up the rope ladder. Rahab's help almost made up for everything else. Almost.

"Girls, come and sit at the table! Let's get to know one another," Rahab called. They squeezed all twelve of them—plus lots of bears and other stuffies—onto the benches around the table. Maddie tried not to be interested in the conversation, but couldn't help it. She found out that Mia's gerbils were having babies. Charlotte's mom had climbed Mt. Everest, and Sarah was working on her black belt in judo. Evelyn and Addison were stepsisters, though they looked nothing alike. Maddie told the group that she never knew who paid for her to go to Camp Liverwurst each summer.

Maddie's cabin leaders also introduced themselves. Priscilla was married, and she and her husband were from Italy. They had helped people learn about Jesus in what is now the country of Turkey.

Rahab preferred to save most of her story for later in the week. "I have much to tell you," she said, "but for now, I will give away only one thing about myself: I am the great-great-great-great-great-great-great-great-great-great-great-great-great (was that enough 'greats'? Probably not!) great-great-great grandmother of Jesus."

Most of the girls gasped and stared. Lizzie broke the silence that followed Rahab's announcement. "But how could you be? You don't even look old enough to be a grandmother!"

Rahab looked at Maddie. "You've been here before, Maddie. Why don't you explain to our newcomers how I can be the many-greats-grandmother of Jesus. My words didn't surprise you, did they?"

"Well, no, but also yes," answered Maddie. "I mean, I get that you're from a long time ago, but it's weird to think of you as a whole-bunch-of-greats-grandmother of Jesus." She turned to the other girls. "Okay, you've noticed that some of the camp leaders have unusual names, right? And you'll discover that Noah has a big boat with many animals, including some that no longer exist. And the camp cook's name is Martha, and Queen Esther is in charge of the games. It's because all the leaders at Camp Liverwurst are Bible characters," Maddie explained. "And they aren't just pretending! Every summer, people from the stories of the Bible appear at the camp, ready to welcome us kids for a week that's... that's out of this world..." She stopped, thinking about how much fun she had in all her past summers at camp. This week had started out so differently.

The girls who had been to Camp Liverwurst before nodded their agreement, but Rylie was skeptical. "Are you saying you're thousands of years old?" she asked Rahab and Priscilla. "Like Galadriel in *The Lord of the Rings?*"

Rahab laughed, which surprised Maddie, who wasn't sure if she could. "No, we lived ordinary lifetimes. But it was a long while ago." She smiled at Rylie's puzzled face. "I'm sorry that I have no explanation for why we're with you at this camp." She looked around at each of them. "But I'm glad we are."

"Who's ready for an awesome week at Camp Liverwurst?" shouted Priscilla. The girls cheered and screamed and gave each other high-fives. Except for Maddie, who sat in her corner with her head down. She didn't see Rahab in the opposite corner, watching her thoughtfully.

4. What Else Could Go Wrong?

Priscilla brought out a cooler full of lunch. She handed a big sub sandwich to each camper, plus chips, potato salad and half a watermelon. Maddie helped herself and went to sit on her bunk.

Where Rylie and Mia were already sitting.

Maddie saw lots of bread crumbs and a splotch of mustard on her sleeping bag. And her pillow was on the floor. "Get off!" she demanded, feet planted in front of them.

"Well, that's not polite," Rylie replied. "We can scotch over; there's lots of room."

"No, get off! You're making a mess of my bed." Maddie and Rylie glared at one another. Mia retreated before something exploded. The conversations in the cabin faltered. After a few moments, Rylie broke eye contact, slowly gathered her lunch and climbed up onto her own bunk. There was a collective sigh of relief in the room, and the voices resumed.

Maddie picked up her pillow, brushed the crumbs off the bed and dabbed up the mustard with a tissue. It still left a mark. She felt tears in the corners of her eyes, but it was herself that she was upset with. Ms. Williams was right—she used to be a happy and thoughtful girl. How did she end up being so grouchy and mean? She laid down on her bunk, pulled her sleeping bag over her, faced the wall and shut out everyone for a while.

In the dark cocoon she had made for herself, Maddie felt the weight of someone sitting down on the edge of her bed. She felt a gentle hand on her shoulder, but the person didn't speak. Maddie's curiosity got the best of her. She lifted her head out of the sleeping bag to look. Priscilla and Ava smiled down at her.

That's when Maddie noticed that, except for Ava and Priscilla, the cabin was empty. "Rahab slipped out with the other girls. I think they're at the climbing gym," Priscilla explained. "How are you feeling, Maddie?"

Maddie sat up and pulled the bag around her. "Like nothing's gone right since I arrived," she said into the sleeping bag. Priscilla couldn't hear what she said, so Maddie looked up and repeated, "Ever since I got here, everything's been horrible!"

Priscilla looked at Maddie for a few moments, like she was reading a book. "Thanks for telling me how you feel, Maddie," she replied. "I know that so far, your time at camp hasn't been the same as other summers. Everything is different this year. But Maddie, is it actually horrible?"

Maddie spoke angrily into her sleeping bag again, loud enough for Priscilla to hear. "Well, then it must be me that's horrible!" She didn't want to cry, especially with Ava there, but she couldn't help it. Priscilla moved beside Maddie and put an arm around her. She said nothing until Maddie's sobs subsided, which took a while. Priscilla asked, "Maddie, can I tell you about a discovery I made?"

Maddie looked up at her. "I guess."

Priscilla handed Maddie her forgotten sub sandwich. "It's not my discovery," she explained. "A leader named Paul, who taught me so much, shared it with me long ago. This guy had been through a lot: he'd been robbed by bandits, thrown in prison, shipwrecked twice, and left for dead. But good things happened too: he traveled the world, he spoke with kings, and he helped many needy people. He told me that through it all, he made a discovery: he discovered how to be content, no matter what happened."

Ava spoke up. "I don't get it. Why was he content when all that bad stuff happened to him?"

"Yeah, I know. It doesn't seem to make sense, does it?" Priscilla answered. "You see, he knew he couldn't stop bad things from happening. All he could change was how he felt about stuff, but that's very hard to do. Then he made the discovery. He could rely on Jesus, who gave him enough strength to be content in his darkest and brightest moments. Since he knew Jesus was trustworthy, my friend was okay even when his ship was going down. He was even thankful!"

Maddie was thinking about this as Priscilla continued, "I tried it out myself. Sometimes I didn't get it right and let my fears and frustrations overwhelm me. But in the times that mattered the most, it was true. Jesus was there, giving me the strength to handle the toughest times and thoroughly enjoy the best of times. That's my hope for you, Maddie. And you too, Ava."

Priscilla stood up, stretched, and held out her hands to Maddie and Ava. "Do you two like rock climbing?" Climbing was one of Maddie's favorites, and she nodded. "Let's go, shall we? I'm sure we have enough time for at least some bouldering."

When they arrived at the gym, it was full of kids climbing walls, navigating overhangs and poking their heads out of caves. Maddie loved this gym. It was all natural rock formations, but she seemed to discover new challenges with each climb. As she was looking around for anybody familiar, a boy on a rappel line landed right in front of her.

"Jayden!" Maddie exclaimed. "Oh, it's such a relief to see someone I know!"

"Hey, Maddie," said Jayden as he removed his rappel device. "How's it going with your new cabin group?" With a thump, Evan landed beside him. Maddie was envious that these two best friends got to be together.

"Not good at all!" Maddie replied. "Hey, Evan," she continued shyly.

"What's not good?" asked Evan as he pulled off his helmet. Maddie's heart fluttered.

"Well, I'm stuck with a group where I don't know anyone," she replied, "and I haven't seen Olivia since the parking lot. And I don't think the girls in my cabin like me." She wanted to change the subject, so she asked, "Weren't you going to some other camp this summer, Evan?"

He laughed. "Yeah, it's a camp not far from my house. The cabins are plywood shacks, and the lake is more like a pond with leeches in it. But I love it! I'm going back as soon as I leave here, and I'll be a junior cabin leader now that my training is over. I can't wait!"

Maddie shuddered at the thought of leeches. "How about you, Jayden?" she asked. "Where did you get your amazing tan?"

"I've been mowing lawns to pay for camp every chance I get," he replied. "I even charge my dad now!" Maddie felt a twinge of guilt. Her time at camp was free, yet she didn't even want to be there.

"Well, Maddie," Evan's voice was confident, "I'm sure your week will turn out great. I mean, it's Camp Liverwurst! What could possibly go wrong?"

Everything—so far, Maddie thought to herself. Out loud, she said, "Thanks, Evan. Like, I won't have to spend all my time with my cabin group. I'm sure we'll get to…"

From across the gym, Rahab's loud voice interrupted her again. "We're leaving, Maddie! Back to the cabin to get ready for dinner. Stay with us, please!"

Maddie sighed. Jayden looked at his watch. "Dinner? It's not for another hour yet…"

His friend Evan dug him in the ribs. "No worries, Maddie. We'll catch up soon. See you around!"

Maddie was not impressed as she followed her group back to the cabin. Once they had all climbed inside, Rahab had them sit at the table again. "I guess you're wondering why we came back early from our activity," she said. "We have something to tell you about. Priscilla?"

The assistant cabin leader grabbed a large backpack from under the table. She reached in and pulled out stuff that Maddie didn't recognize. "Let me see… camp stove—check! Ice axe—check! Crampons—check! First aid kit—check!" She smiled at the girls and said, "Anyone guess what it's all for? That's right—we're going camping! We leave tomorrow morning, and we will be out on the trail for two nights!"

Maddie couldn't believe her ears! Away from even the hope of seeing her friends for three of her six remaining days at Camp Liverwurst? Camping with strangers who didn't like her? Maddie couldn't imagine anything worse!

She found Olivia's table at dinnertime and described her *terrible, horrible, no good, very bad day.* "We had to pack up all our stuff in these big, heavy backpacks. We even have to carry the food we'll eat, and I have part of a tent and a pot in my bag. I won't be able to walk one block with all that on my back!"

"I don't know," replied Olivia. "It sounds kinda fun! I wish I could go with you."

"That would be the best!" Maddie exclaimed. "I wouldn't mind so much if you were there. Do you think she would let you…" She broke off as Rahab pulled out a chair and sat at their table.

"Hey, Maddie," she said, smiling. "Who's your friend?"

Maddie introduced her to Olivia, who said, "Maddie was telling me about your camping trip. I love camping!"

"Camping is good," Rahab agreed. "Even God enjoys camping. When I joined the people of Israel, I discovered that the entire nation went camping with God for one week each year." She looked at Maddie. "But this experience is more about the trip than the camping. I believe it will be an important journey for our cabin group."

So much for Olivia coming along, thought Maddie. Olivia asked Rahab, "Where exactly are you going?"

"Maddie hasn't told you?" Rahab looked surprised. "We will climb Mount Hermon! Well, not the real Mount Hermon in Israel—that would take too much rowing—but a mountain nearby that reminds us of it because there is always snow at the top. The prophet wrote, 'Does the snow of Lebanon ever leave the crags of Hermon?' " She laughed when she saw the shocked looks on the girls' faces. "Yes, we will hike in the snow!"

5. Someone Knows Who I Am

"Snow?" Maddie spluttered. "But… but it's summer-time! We're supposed to be, I don't know, swimming and stuff. We didn't pack clothes for snow."

"Trust me, Maddie, we will be fine," Rahab assured her. "The mountain will be not much colder than here, and we have hiking boots and other gear for each of you."

The dining room grew suddenly quiet as a lovely lady, who Maddie knew as Queen Esther, commanded everyone's attention with the microphone. "Welcome to Camp Liverwurst!" she shouted.

The campers went wild with screaming and cheering. Some of them chanted, "Quee-nie! Quee-nie! Quee-nie!" and she laughed.

"Who is at Camp Liverwurst for the first time?" Queen Esther asked. Maddie was surprised at how many hands went up. Several of them were her new cabinmates. "That means the rest of you have a responsibility of love—to make the new ones feel at home and help them find their way. Will you do that for me?" Lots of cheers.

Maddie realized it had never occurred to her to find out who was new and to offer them help. She was focused on her own disappointments and hadn't remembered what it was like to be at camp for the first time. Ava, who was sitting at the table across from her, had raised her hand as a new camper. But Ava was the first person to make Maddie feel welcome. Maddie wished it was the other way around.

"I'm so hungry, I could eat a unicorn!" Queen Esther shouted. "Don't worry, Noah, I won't." Unlike most of the campers, Maddie didn't laugh. Queen Esther said a few words of thanks to God for the meal, and the campers dug into the lasagna like they hadn't eaten for a week.

As they were eating, Maddie glanced at her cabin leader and asked Olivia, "Hey, do you know who my cabin leader Rahab is?"

Olivia cautiously answered, "Yeah, I kinda do…" Maddie wondered why she looked concerned about it. "But you tell me."

Maddie said, "She's the great-great-great-great-great-great… Was that enough greats?" Rahab smiled and shook her head. "Anyway, lots of greats-grandmother of Jesus!"

"Really?" replied Olivia, surprised. "I didn't know that! I wouldn't have thought…" She stopped, embarrassed. Rahab looked up at her sharply with a quizzical look on her face.

"Wouldn't have thought what?" asked Maddie, looking at them both.

"Nothing," replied Olivia, eyes on her plate. "It's nothing; don't worry about it." They continued eating in silence.

"Dessert, anyone?" Maddie turned to see who was asking and nearly squeaked with excitement. It was Abigail, her old cabin leader. Abigail set down her tray of apple pies to give Maddie a hug. "And I hear you have a special adventure planned for them, Rahab. So fun!"

"Yes, I'm sure we will have fun," Rahab agreed. "However, we'll also face difficulties and challenges. We can't expect only enjoyment, can we?" She took the slice of pie Abigail handed her. "Weren't we always at our best because of a difficult time, when everything seemed hopeless?"

"You're right, Rahab!" answered Abigail. She took a piece of pie from the tray and sat down to join them. "We both had to do some hard things to respond to those difficulties, didn't we? But look at who we became because of it!"

Maddie didn't like this conversation. "Um, this is a kid's camp! Like, where we play games and sing crazy songs and eat great food. What's with all this talk about hardship?"

"Fair enough, Maddie," Abigail replied. "But this is also life, and you never know what is ahead of you." She smiled. "But you can know *who* is ahead of you."

Maddie had heard her say this before and knew she was talking about Jesus. She liked the idea that Jesus is with us in our difficult times, but why did he let those bad things happen in the first place? As if reading her thoughts, Rahab said, "Yes, there is no hardship or temptation that Jesus hasn't already experienced. He leads the way."

After another silence, Olivia broke in, "Well, this apple pie is no hardship! It's the best ever! Maddie, if you're not going to finish that…" Maddie slid her plate over to her friend and saw everyone getting up from their tables. "Chapel time, right?" Maddie exclaimed. She looked at Rahab and said, "Would you mind if I…"

Rahab finished her thought. "You can sit wherever you want in chapel tonight, Maddie. I know you like to be with your friends. See you back at the cabin afterward."

Olivia gobbled down Maddie's pie, and they raced off to join the others climbing the stairs. The big room at the top was an open space except for cushions all over the floor and musical instruments at the front. As they entered, the band started playing the kind of music that makes you want to get up and move your feet. Miriam grabbed the microphone and shouted, "Who's ready to make a joyful noise to the Lord?" The crowd was deafening! Words showed up on the wall, and the campers sang:

Here is what he said to me
The One who made me
The One who shaped me
Here is what he said to me
The day I lost my way
Do not be afraid
I have found you!
I have paid your bill
I have called you by name!
When you cross the water

I will be there
When you ford the rivers
They will not overwhelm you
Blazing forests
Won't even singe your hair!
For I am the Lord your God
The Holy One of Israel
The One who saves you
And I have called you by name!

After several songs like it, they fell panting onto the cushions. Maddie loved the music, but the words troubled her. She wished she knew—really knew—if God was there. An older man got up to speak. Maddie smiled as she recognized his yellow pants, yellow shirt, yellow hat and polka-dot tie. "Good evening, everyone!" he said. "My name is Moses, and I always have the privilege of telling you the camp rules. However, I trust in your ability to read (or be read to), so I have posted the rules on the doorpost of your cabin…"

Olivia poked Maddie and whispered, "Joke's on him! Your cabin doesn't have a doorpost!" Maddie laughed.

Moses continued, "Tonight, I will only remind you of the two most important rules of all time, at camp and everywhere: Love God, love people." He chuckled, "Sounds simple, right? But these rules are the hardest of all. We love God by trusting that he knows what is best for us. And we love people by treating them like we want to be treated. Not easy at all! But we have a great big God who is for us, not against us, and he will help. Have a wonderful week!"

After a few more songs, Miriam introduced the speaker for the evening. "Hey, everyone," she called out, "give a huge welcome to someone who has some important words for us." A woman with a kind face joined her at the front. "You know her as Mary, but we like to call her 'Mom.' "

When the crowd settled down, Mary spoke in a quiet and compelling voice. The campers leaned in to hear her. "Every time…" she began, and closed her eyes. "Every time I am given an opportunity like this, my heart says, Why me? Who am I that God has done such great things for me? Holy is his name!"

She was quiet for several moments. Mary opened her eyes and looked around at the group of campers. "How beautiful all of you are, and how proud your parents should be of you! As I was proud of him, Jesus the Messiah, my son."

Maddie heard campers gasp around her, and she smiled to herself. She remembered how hard it was at first to believe that the leaders at camp were people from the Bible. Even now, she wondered if it was true. Could this woman be the great-great-great-plus-a-lot-of greats granddaughter of her cabin leader, Rahab?

Mary told the story of an angel who came to tell her she would be the mother of Jesus. "Think of me," she said, "a poor girl, not much older than you, who trusted in God and brought his Son into the world. I expected to live an ordinary life in my small, ordinary village. But God stepped in and made my life extraordinary."

She smiled at them. "There is a word for this. To some of you, it is not a familiar word, and others may not understand what it means. The word is 'blessing.' It is all about blossoming life and abundant goodness. My ancestor Abraham... Hi, Abraham!" She waved to a man standing at the back, leaning on a broom. "God promised to bless Abraham so that through him all the world would be blessed.

"His promise also came through others in this room, including Rahab and your worship leader, David. And finally, through me. I conceived—I don't know how, not in the usual way—and gave birth to a beautiful baby boy. I wrapped him in clean rags and laid him in a manger. I was blessed by God so that I could be a blessing to the world.

"Many of you are struggling with the question of who you are, your identity. I feel for you! It is a hard question." That's for sure, Maddie said to herself. Mary continued, "I can't answer the question for you, but I know someone who has known the answer since before the world was formed. He says you are his masterpiece; you are one of a kind. His desire is to bless you so that you can be a blessing to the world. And his name is Jesus."

Mary continued talking for a while, but Maddie's mind was racing. Ms. Williams had said she first figured out who she was when she realized who Jesus is. If Jesus created me, and if I am his work of art, he knows who I am. Hope leaped up in Maddie's heart, then stumbled and tumbled down. She thought about her dad, who believed we are only a beautiful accident. Who was right? The two ideas simply couldn't be true at the same time.

6. A Person to Follow

Maddie was so deep in thought as she left chapel that she walked straight into a circle of older girls from another cabin. One of them pushed her away and said in disgust, "Don't touch me, you little tramp!"

Maddie looked up at her, startled by her words. "Huh? What do you mean?"

"You're from that… that woman's cabin, right?" She said it like she wanted to say something else but didn't dare.

"You mean Rahab? So what?" Maddie found herself defending the cabin leader she didn't like.

"So, don't you know who she is? You should be embarrassed to be in a cabin with someone like her! My mom would never let me. Your cabin leader is a… well, she's a very, very bad person."

"How do you know?" Maddie demanded.

"Read your Bible, you ignorant heathen!" All the girls laughed as they walked away.

Maddie was furious, but troubled too. She stood there, shaking with anger, waiting so she wouldn't run into those girls again. She had to go find Olivia. Maddie turned to leave the chapel.

And found herself face-to-face with Rahab.

Maddie didn't know what to say. Had Rahab heard what those girls said about her? Rahab put a hand on her shoulder. "Are you okay, Maddie? You look upset."

Face turning red, Maddie replied, "Um, just some girls being mean. It's nothing; I can deal with it."

"Well, come," Rahab said. "Let's walk back to the cabin together and join the others. We have an early start tomorrow. Plus, I have a question to ask you. And something to give you." Maddie would have rather talked with Olivia. But she was curious about what Rahab had for her.

They walked in silence along the waterfront. Tinges of red still lingered in the sky, reflecting on the lake. Finally, Rahab stopped and asked, "Maddie, have you ever thought of yourself as a leader?"

Her question surprised Maddie. "No! Not ever. I don't… I don't know why anyone would ever want to follow me."

"Well, it's true—leaders need followers," Rahab agreed. "But you may not realize who is following you even now, at camp."

"Really?" Maddie replied. "I can't think of anyone. There's nobody in my cabin group, that's for sure. They don't even like me!"

"Now it's my turn to say, 'Really?' " said Rahab. "I know you had a small tiff with Rylie. But I have never heard the girls say anything negative about you. Sometimes they ask where you are." Rahab took something from her pocket and held it out to Maddie. "I would like you to have this." It was a small metal case. Maddie opened it and saw that it was a compass.

She looked up at Rahab, who asked her, "What does this do, Maddie?"

"Well, it always points north," Maddie answered. "People use a compass to find their way."

"That's exactly right. A compass can be a valuable instrument for people who have strayed from their path," said Rahab. "Maddie, I believe you are a compass." They began walking again. "I want you to think about what it takes to become someone whom others want to follow. We can talk about this more on the camping trip. Sound okay?"

"I guess," Maddie answered. "It's sure not something I ever thought about before." She paused and said, "Thank you, Rahab." Her cabin leader hugged her, and they walked to the cabin in silence. Maddie suddenly had a lot to think about.

The girls were excited about the camping trip in the morning, which made it difficult for them to settle down that night. Priscilla told them stories of places she had traveled by boat, on foot and once on a camel, which she said was the worst of all. "But we won't find camels where we're going! Maybe mountain goats." That's what Maddie dreamed about that night—hairy goats scooping cones from a mountain made of huckleberry ice cream.

The sun was rising when Rahab and Priscilla woke them. "You go on ahead, I'll catch up," mumbled Lizzy as she rolled over and went back to sleep. Breakfast was bowls of crunchy granola that Priscilla handed out. The campers heaped yogurt and huckleberries on top. "I could eat this all day!" said Maddie. "Thanks, Priscilla!"

The other girls looked surprised to hear her cheerful words, which added to the strange warmth Maddie felt inside.

When the campers had cleaned up, they lowered their backpacks from the window and climbed down the red ladder after them. For the first few minutes, Maddie's pack felt very uncomfortable. She was thankful when Rahab adjusted her shoulder straps and hip belt.

But she wasn't expecting her leaders to take them to the dock. "Stow your backpacks in the bottom of the boat, girls!" Rahab instructed. "Keep the weight low, and that will make us more stable. We'll row a distance down the lake. From there, we can access the river valley that will lead us to the mountain." Maddie sighed. Her hands were still sore from rowing to the camp yesterday. She wasn't thrilled about getting back in the boat. Hopefully, it was a quick trip.

But it wasn't. What's more, the lake was far from calm that day. A playful wind swirled around them, making the water choppy. Before long, everyone had been splashed, either by a wave or an oar that missed the water. Rahab directed the boat into a calm bay sheltered from the wind. The girls collapsed on their oars with a groan. "It's not far now, girls! Keep up your good pace, and we'll be there in no time!"

Easy for you to say, Maddie thought to herself. Rahab just had to sit and steer while the campers did all the hard work of rowing. It wasn't fair! "I'd like to see you do it," Maddie mumbled to herself, or so she thought. But Rahab heard what she said.

50

"Maddie, are you saying you want to trade places with me?" Rahab asked.

"Um, I guess! Yeah, I *do* want to trade places with you." Part of her mind was shouting, What are you thinking? But anger took over. "I don't see why we should do all the rowing and you and Priscilla just sit there!"

"Think carefully, Maddie," Rahab cautioned. "Do you want to take responsibility for the safety of all your cabinmates and leaders? This may be more challenging than you think."

"It looks pretty easy to me!" Maddie countered.

"Okay, I don't mind taking a turn rowing," Rahab replied. "But you must follow Priscilla's commands. Remember, the best leader is the one who has learned to be the best follower. Pay close attention to what you're doing, especially with the wind picking up. We're counting on you, Maddie!"

Balancing carefully so she didn't rock the boat, Maddie traded places with Rahab. The seat at the stern of the boat was higher than where the rowers sat. It was cool to see everyone looking up at her. But Maddie soon realized that her slightest movement affected the balance for everyone. She could see why she had to pay attention.

The boat moved out of the bay as Priscilla gave commands to the rowers. "A little to starboard, Maddie," she called. Maddie adjusted the steering oar, but the boat turned to port instead of starboard. She quickly adjusted in the other direction, making the boat wobble a bit. Finally, she had the boat moving in a straight line. See? Easy, she said to herself.

They left the calm bay and entered the waves. Immediately, the steering oar tugged back and forth. It took everything she had to keep the boat moving straight. "Are you okay, Maddie?" Rahab called.

"Yep, I'm fine!" Maddie didn't feel fine, but she didn't want to look like a loser in front of the other girls. She gritted her teeth and held on. The boat was moving pretty fast with the wind now at her back. Maddie noticed that when a larger wave came up behind them, the stern of the boat wanted to shift sideways. It took all her strength to keep it straight.

"Maddie!" Priscilla called from the other end of the boat. "Steer the boat down the waves. Don't let us turn broadside—like, sideways—to the waves. It could make us capsize." Great, Maddie thought. That would sure make her unpopular with these girls! When the next big wave came up from behind, she steered to port. The boat rode down the wave for a moment before it passed under them. "Well done, Maddie!" Priscilla called. "We're surfing!"

Now Maddie was having fun. She almost hoped for huge waves because it felt cool to ride them. But steering the boat took lots of concentration. She looked up and saw they were entering a wide bay. Soon, she could see all the way up a thickly-forested valley to where an enormous mountain towered above the hills. She realized she was the only one in the boat who could see all this, since everyone else was facing her.

"Hey, is that Mount Hermon?" Maddie shouted. All the girls stopped rowing and turned around to look. A few of them kneeled on their seats to see the mountain better.

That's when it happened. A massive wave came up behind them. "Maddie, watch your steering!" Priscilla shouted. Maddie reached for her forgotten steering oar and tried to turn the boat down the wave. The oar felt like a live thing and wriggled out of its thole pins. Losing her balance, Maddie desperately clutched the stern of the boat. Over it went as the wave lifted them broadside and threw campers, leaders and their backpacks into the lake.

7. A Change of Plans

All around Maddie, there was a confusion of waves and screams and panicking campers. "Everyone, calm down!" Rahab shouted. "Grab a backpack and swim toward the sound of my voice. I want everyone to stay together!"

Maddie clung to the backpack floating nearest to her and tried to spot Rahab. She found Lizzy looking wildly around her and said, "Hold on to this backpack and come with me. I'll find another one." She pulled both Lizzy and the backpack along until she found another nearby. Maddie saw a cluster of campers and figured that must be where they would find Rahab.

When she spotted them, Rahab was saying, "…and Charlotte and Sarah, and—oh, thank God, here's Maddie and Lizzie. That's everyone!"

"Except for our boat," said Rylie. She was right. Maddie couldn't see the boat anywhere.

"Don't worry about the boat," said Priscilla. "She's made of wood, so she won't sink. She's a tough old dory! They'll find her washed up on a beach somewhere."

"Did everyone grab a backpack?" Rahab asked. "No? How many do we have?" After a clamor of counting, they agreed that only two backpacks were missing. "Hopefully not the ones with the toilet paper," Rahab laughed. "Okay, we'll start moving toward the beach. Let's take our time and help one another. Stay close together, everyone!"

Their progress through the water was slow. But the beach was not far from where they capsized. The warm sun was high in the sky, and the wind and waves grew calmer. The girls laughed and chattered as they floated in their life vests in the cool water. It was Maddie and Rylie who helped Rahab and Priscilla keep their raft of campers moving toward the shore.

Finally, Maddie felt gravel beneath her feet. She and Rylie and their leaders pulled all the girls and backpacks along as the water became shallower. Maddie shouted, "Hey, everyone, stand up!" The girls stopped their chatter in surprise and stood up, laughing. Soon, everyone and their gear were sprawled out on a soft and sunny beach made of tiny round gravel like you might find in a playground.

"Well, that was an adventure!" said Priscilla. "First things first! Let's get dried out as best we can. Shoes and socks off! Lay everything you can on the warm gravel to dry. Rahab and I will deal with your packs." Some things had stayed dry in the backpacks, but the campers hung several sleeping bags and lots of clothes on branches and driftwood. Soon, the whole beach looked like an outdoor thrift shop.

The campers were happy to hear that the toilet paper had survived. Most of the food was well-packaged and safe. "But not the trail mix!" moaned

Sarah. She held up a soggy bag of dried fruit, nuts and chocolate chips. "That's disgusting!"

Rahab opened the bag of trail mix and looked inside. "We can salvage this!" she said. "Maddie, see if you can find a tarp or tent fly in one of the backpacks." Maddie remembered a roll of fabric and went to retrieve it. Priscilla helped Maddie open the tarp on a sunny part of the beach. Rahab poured several bags of mushy trail mix all over the tarp and spread it out.

"I'm not eating that!" Addison exclaimed, and all the girls agreed with her.

"We'll see," replied Rahab. "Once it's dry, maybe we can make something with it." She looked around at the cluttered beach. "And while everything is drying out, let's hold a council and decide what we will do." They found a space on the beach to sit in a circle. Maddie wondered if they would continue the journey with missing backpacks and no boat for their return.

"Well, girls," Rahab began, "this is not the adventure we expected, but it's the one we are given. What will we do with it?" She pointed up the valley to where the tip of the mountain peeked out. "Maddie was correct. That is Mount Hermon, and we've landed on the beach where we intended to begin our trek. So far, so good. However, we're missing some of our supplies. The GPS device we could have used to call for help was in Priscilla's pack, which is one of the two we lost. Plus, we have no means of getting back to Camp Liverwurst. Not by water, anyway."

The girls had lots of ideas and questions. "Can't we walk back along the shore?" "Maybe our boat will wash up on the beach!" "Shouldn't we be calling 9-1-1?" Maddie asked a question that made the rest of the girls go quiet. "What's stopping us from doing what we came to do? Let's climb the mountain!"

Maddie couldn't believe the words coming out of her mouth. Until now, she had only wished she was back at camp. And it was her fault they were in this predicament. But now that they were here, a spirit of adventure was growing inside her. She wanted to reach the top of the mountain!

The girls all burst out at once. "My sleeping bag is wet!" "We won't have enough food!" "I'm not eating garbage off a tarp!" Rylie stood and glared at Maddie and said, "You got us into this mess, Maddie! Now get us out of it!"

Everyone was on their feet and talking at once. Priscilla shouted above the crowd, "Girls, stop talking by the time I count to three. One! Two! Three!" The clamor died down and left Maddie and Rylie glaring at one another.

Rahab spoke in a calm voice. "Girls, we have to face the fact that we have no easy way home. Blaming someone won't help; really, all of us made the boat capsize." Everyone sat down in the circle again. Rahab unfolded a large map with lots of squiggly lines and laid it out on the beach. "This is a topographic map, and the lines show the elevation. These V's indicate the valley next to us, and the squares are Mt. Hermon." She ran her finger along the valley. "Here is our route, marked by a dotted line. Along the valley and up this ridge. But what do you see at the top of the mountain?"

"Another dotted line, going the other direction," answered Ava. "Does that mean there's another way to climb the mountain?"

"Yes," replied Rahab, "and it leads all the way back to camp. But the trail is longer and more challenging, which is why we decided to use the boat and take this route instead. And no," she said to Lizzie before she finished asking, "it's not possible to walk along the shore back to the camp. The shoreline is much too thick and steep."

Maddie spoke up. "All we have to do is climb the mountain from this side and take the other trail back to the camp? What are we waiting for?" This seemed like a no-brainer to Maddie. She would get to climb the mountain and also return to camp.

"It's not as easy as it seems, Maddie," Rahab replied. "For one thing, we landed on the wrong side of the river that flows down the valley. It will be challenging to cross to the other side. And, as I said before, the trail from the mountain to the camp is long and parts are quite difficult."

"We can do it!" Maddie exclaimed. "What do you think, everyone? Who's up for climbing the mountain and walking back to Camp Liverwurst?" A few of the girls shot up their hands in response to Maddie's enthusiasm, but others looked uncertain. A couple of campers moaned, and one said, "I want my mom!"

"So much for that idea, Maddie!" Rylie sneered.

"Thank you for all of your ideas, girls!" Rahab intervened. "But none of us knows what is the best way to return safely to camp. The problem is that we've forgotten to consult with the only One who does know. We're like a flock of sheep, each wanting to go her own way. Let's talk with our Shepherd!"

Rahab stood, raised her arms in the air and prayed, "Jesus, you are the Good Shepherd, and you care about us more than anyone does. Thank you for this unexpected adventure. Thank you for getting us safely to a sunny beach, along with most of our gear and food." She began clapping her hands, and all the girls joined her.

She continued, "God, please show us the best way to return everyone safely to Camp Liverwurst. You know the strengths and limitations of every girl here. I pray that each one will use her strengths well and be content with her limitations. Please tell one of us what we should do. We ask in the name of Jesus, Amen."

When she finished, the girls were quiet. Rahab sat down again and said, "Well, we have asked the only Person who knows what we should do. Let's trust him and expect him to provide an answer. In fact, I believe he will give the answer to one of you." The girls looked at one another, wondering who it would be. "In the meantime, we have work to do! Check all your things and see if they are completely dry. Pack up anything that is. I'll see what we can do about the trail mix."

The girls scampered around, checking clothes and sleeping bags, turning things over or inside out to dry more. Priscilla and a few campers gathered driftwood and built a fire. Maddie joined Rahab, who was examining the tarp covered in trail mix. "It looks dry," observed Rahab, "but the chocolate chips are melting.

That gives me an idea, Maddie! Please bring me our biggest pot and the bowls stacked up inside it."

Rahab and Maddie carefully poured all the gooey trail mix into the empty pot. It looked pretty awful. Rahab set the pot near the fire and gave Maddie a big spoon. "Keep stirring it, okay? Don't stop," she instructed. "Call me as soon as it's all melted together." Maddie sat for some time, stirring the sticky mess and trying to keep the smoke from getting in her eyes. Lots of thoughts kept whirling around in her mind. But soon, one thought came into clearer and clearer focus. When the trail mix looked like cake batter, Maddie called Rahab, who was helping a camper turn her sleeping bag inside out. "This looks perfect, Maddie!" she said. They poured and scooped the batter into each of the soup bowls and set them in the shade with a towel over them.

When they were done, Maddie got up her courage. "Rahab, I think I know what God wants us to do."

"I believe you, Maddie," Rahab replied. "I'm not at all surprised that you're the one he chose to tell. What do you believe we should do?"

Maddie gulped. This was so much responsibility! "We don't all need to walk up the mountain and down to the camp. Some should stay here, and a small group of us should make the trek and bring help." Maddie knew in her heart that this was the right thing to do. But "a small group of us" meant she needed to be one of the people to go!

8. The Rescue Party

Rahab gathered the girls again and asked Maddie to tell them her plan. "I don't know who should make the hike," Maddie said, "except… well, I think I'm supposed to be one of them."

"Why?" demanded Rylie.

"I just know, somehow," Maddie replied. "It's hard to explain. I know it won't be easy. I think we need to decide together who should make up our rescue team."

The girls talked for several minutes. Priscilla and Rahab watched and listened. In the end, the girls decided that Maddie, Ava, Mia and Rylie should go. Maddie looked at Rahab and Priscilla. "And who will…?"

"Rahab's coming with you," said Priscilla. "I'll stay and set up camp with the rest of the girls and await our rescue. But I'm afraid we'll have more fun than the five of you!"

"That's likely true," Rahab agreed. "Are you four girls sure you're up to the challenge?"

"Let's get started!" Rylie exclaimed.

"We need to decide what to bring with us," said Maddie.

"You'll need some of these, at least." Priscilla took a bowl of trail mix goop and lifted out a perfectly formed disc of hard chocolate loaded with dried fruit and nuts.

"Yum, I want one right now!" said Lizzie. "Let's call them 'Hermon Bars'! " The girls laughed.

"It's no longer tarp garbage," Priscilla chuckled. "But we don't know how long we will be here. We'll have to ration our food carefully, not eat it all at once."

Rahab helped the four hikers decide what they needed to bring with them. They took all the essentials but packed as lightly as possible. The girls decided they could squeeze into one tent. They brought sleeping bags and mats, no pillows, and only one change of warmer clothes. Priscilla divided the food they would need among them, and they loaded everything into one backpack each.

"This will be easy!" Rylie lifted her pack without effort.

"Not so fast," cautioned Rahab. She handed out several items they hadn't thought of. Spiked traction devices to attach to their boots for walking on snow and ice. A length of climbing rope, climbing equipment and harnesses. A small pot and a stove. Headlamps and sunscreen. Soon, their packs were not so light anymore.

"Make sure your water bottles are full," Rahab instructed. "Each of you needs to find a solid branch as tall as you; I'll let you know if it's suitable. And we'll have lunch together before we leave."

Soon, the four hikers and their leader were ready to go. The girls and Priscilla gathered around, and

Priscilla prayed for them. "Father in heaven," she said, "You are good and you love us. Please walk with Maddie, Rylie, Ava, Mia and Rahab on the trail. Keep them well and keep them safe. And give them success on their journey up the mountain and to the camp so someone can rescue us." All the girls said, Amen!

The hikers first walked along the beach toward the place where the river cut through it. With their backpacks on, the soft gravel felt like walking in deep snow. They were glad when Rahab led them to firmer ground along the riverbank. "The water is too deep and fast by the beach," she explained. "We need a safe place to ford the river so we can find the trail on the other side."

They soon came to a spot where the river was wider and ran noisily over the rocks. "Will this do?" asked Maddie, who was at the front of the group. Rahab agreed and showed them how they would get across, using the sturdy branches they had brought with them. She stood in the water facing upstream, feet wide apart, and leaned on her branch so she looked like a tripod.

When Rylie tried it next, she shrieked, "Yikes! The water is icy cold! I thought about taking off my boots to keep them dry, but no way!" Soon, they shuffled across the river after their leader, Maddie last. The river was so cold that it hurt. The water flowed nearly to Maddie's knees, and small boulders rolled under her feet. But her tripod stance always kept Maddie from slipping down the stream.

They were soon across. Everyone emptied their soaked boots and wrung out their socks. It wasn't pleasant to put them back on again. "Our boots will dry as we walk," Rahab told them. "But it will be easy to get blisters. As soon as you notice a spot on your foot that's a tiny bit sore, let me know. I have tape that will keep it from becoming a problem."

The route up the valley was breathtakingly beautiful. Massive trunks of fir and cedar trees towered above them on either side, surrounded by moss and ferns. In places, tall purple and pink flowers that Rahab called "lupines" carpeted the forest floor. The air was cool and still, and the only sound was the rushing river.

That is, until Rahab began belting out a Camp Liverwurst song at the top of her lungs. The girls soon caught on because whenever they came to the end, Rahab and Maddie started it up again:

Let's make some noise!
Joyful noise to our God!
Let's make some noise!
Sing and laugh out loud!
Because God is God (not us!)
He made us, we didn't make him
We are his sheep (bah, bah!)
And he's the Shepherd
Not the other way around
Enter his gates with gratefulness
Walk through his courtyard with praise
Thank him before you get there
He will be so happy to see us
Because God is good
His love lasts forever
He's our faithful friend!

"If there's any bear, wolf or cougar around, they'll be long gone after that!" laughed Rahab. "Even Skookum the Sasquatch is probably running for his cave right now."

Maddie looked up at the giant trees. She felt like they had actually entered God's gates and were walking through his courtyard lined with living pillars. In a place like this, it was difficult not to believe in God. Everything was magnificent, fit for a King. She felt grateful, and the only person she could think of to be thankful to was the Maker of it all. How could this marvel possibly be an accident?

The trail became steeper. Huge, mossy boulders lay scattered between the trees, a few as big as houses. Maddie's shoulders were getting sore from the pack straps. She tightened the belt to place more weight on her hips, but her legs became tired. After a while, everything hurt. She was glad when Rahab left the trail toward a small meadow and took off her pack. All the girls did the same and collapsed on the soft turf.

"You're doing well, girls!" Rahab assured them. "We will slow down the pace as we ascend the ridge. Many zigzags up ahead!" She had them remove their boots and socks to check for potential blisters, and she applied thin fabric tape to sore spots.

The meadow was warm and filled with the burbling of a crystal-clear brook. After a snack and a drink from their bottles, the girls sprawled out on the grass and would have been asleep in minutes. "Time to move on, girls!" Rahab encouraged them. "We have a stretch of uphill before we reach the ridge where we'll camp for the night."

"Do we have to?" moaned Mia. "It's so comfortable here. I don't want to move!"

"Then you would have been happier staying with the rest of the girls at the lake," snapped Maddie. "You signed up for this!"

"Leave her alone," Rylie said in defense of her friend. "You got us into this mess!"

"Unkind words won't make our situation any better, girls," warned Rahab. "We'll need to help and depend on one another many times before our journey ends." She pulled Mia to her feet. "I feel what you're feeling, Mia! This is a wonderfully pleasant spot. I could rest here all day. But we need to get walking again."

The way was steep and rocky. Every time the trail zigged or zagged, Maddie thought for sure it would be the last time before they reached the top of the ridge. But there was always another turn and another. Her pack felt like she was carrying a sleeping elephant. When she was sure she could not manage one more zig (and certainly not another zag), the group came suddenly out of the trees onto the ridge.

Before them spread a broad meadow covered in wildflowers of every color and variety. Beyond the meadow were waves of forested hills and valleys as far as the eye could see. The bright blue water of the lake was far below. They couldn't believe how far they had walked! And above the meadow loomed the snowy peak of Mount Hermon. Their eyes couldn't grasp it all with one glance.

"This trip keeps getting better and better," exclaimed Maddie. "I wish the other girls could see this." She didn't notice Rahab's eyes light up when she said it, or her thoughtful look. "It's almost too much to take in."

Rylie agreed for once. "Yeah, I feel like the mountain is about to fall on our heads!"

It wasn't difficult to find a great camping spot with a view. They set up the tent, which looked small for five people, and put their sleeping bags inside. "We'll have more room if we go head to toe," Rahab suggested. They laid out three bags one way and two bags between them the other way, with Rahab in the middle. It was perfect because when they sat up, it was like sitting in a circle.

As they ate dinner, the sun set behind the mountains, turning the meadow into gold. Rahab told them stories about her life in the Middle East. Maddie's heart sank as she remembered the mean words the girls at camp had said about her leader. Surely they couldn't be true.

Ava suddenly called out, "Oh! Look at the mountain!" They turned around. The snow of Mount Hermon was lit up like a bright pink ice cream cone from the waning light of the sun. They watched in silence as the mountain grew even brighter in contrast to the darkening sky behind it. When the last of the light faded, they all sighed. It was far too beautiful for words.

9. Couldn't Have Been More Wrong

Maddie was perfectly warm except for her nose. It was the only part of her sticking out of the sleeping bag, and it felt like it had grown icicles. She sat up. The other girls still slept in their cocoons, but Rahab and her bag were gone. Being careful not to wake the rest, Maddie opened the tent zipper and peered out. Rahab was sitting on a rock close by, still in her sleeping bag. She motioned for Maddie to join her.

The meadow lay in the deep shadow of the mountain. Below them, the forests and the lake were already bathed in golden sunlight. Rahab poured Maddie a cup of hot chocolate from the pot on the tiny camp stove. Maddie wrapped her icy hands around the warm cup and sipped its heavenly contents. She wondered how she could ever not want to come on this trip.

"Thank you!" she whispered, and Rahab smiled. "Not just for the hot chocolate, which is the best ever, by the way. Thank you for taking us here, and for... for putting up with my grumpiness."

"You don't know how glad I am that you are in my cabin group, Maddie," Rahab replied. They sat for a while, sipping their cups and watching the shadows move down the hills as the sun climbed. Finally, Maddie got up her courage.

"Rahab, the other day—at camp—did you hear what those girls were saying about you after chapel?"

Rahab took a sip and replied, "Yes, I did. I've heard that sort of thing said about me often. But I was sad that they called you names because of me."

"They were so mean!" Maddie realized she had said it too loudly and lowered her voice. "But I don't believe them. I can't imagine you ever being a bad person— well, now that I know you better."

Rahab looked at her. "But Maddie, it's true. I was the kind of person that no mom would ever want as a cabin leader for their daughter."

"I don't understand," replied Maddie, her heart sinking.

Rahab looked at the valley below for several moments before answering. "I grew up in a city that was not kind to the poor. And we were very poor. Our house was part of the city wall. From an early age, I had to work to help support my family. I was forced to do many bad things, and as I grew older, I kept doing them to support myself. I was sure it was impossible to escape who I had become.

"Then we heard that another nation was moving into our territory. We were all terrified because we heard how their God had rescued them from slavery in Egypt..."

"He divided the Red Sea for them!" Maddie interjected. "I saw the movie!"

"Yes, and he did many other impossible things for them. Anyway, two men came to my door one night, which would not have been unusual except they were spies from this nation. I was about to alert the leaders in my city, but I had a thought. Their God had rescued them from slavery; perhaps he could rescue me as well. So I hid them and told our leaders they had escaped. Later that night, I lowered a rope from my window so they could climb down the city wall…"

"Oh! That's why you have a rope ladder for your cabin!"

"Yes, it's become a habit of mine. Before they left, the men promised to rescue me and my family. I hung a red rope out of my window so they could find me when they returned. And they did. I joined their nation, which treated the poor better, and I never returned to the bad things I did before. I married a wonderful man, and we had several children and many happy years together."

"So you're not such a bad person after all!" Maddie exclaimed.

Rahab answered, "For a long time, I was one kind of person, and I thought that was all I was. Then I placed myself at the mercy of a God I didn't know and who terrified me. He made me into a new person, and now I know—this is who I truly am. And I love him very much. I was no accident; I was not something to be used and thrown away." She shook her head in wonder. "Maddie, through me, God sent his Son into the world!"

Maddie's mind swirled with thoughts. This was why Olivia was surprised to hear that Rahab was an ancestor of Jesus. That God would choose someone like her was more than surprising. To Maddie, it was beautiful. This was a God who was not happy with those mean girls' attitude. This God takes nobodies and turns them into somebodies. It gave Maddie such a flood of hope that she could hardly contain it.

"Rahab, I love you!" Maddie gave her cabin leader a sleeping bag hug. "When you first told me you were my cabin leader, I was disappointed and angry. But I couldn't have been more wrong about you."

Rahab hugged her back and stretched. "Time to wake the other girls, Maddie! Why don't you serve each of them a cup of hot chocolate in bed? After all, that's what leaders do!"

By the time the girls finished raving over their hot chocolate and stuffing away their sleeping bags, Rahab had a big pot of oatmeal ready to serve. Rylie looked disgusted when she saw it, but was soon gulping it down like the rest. Rahab had sweetened the porridge with maple sugar and had even broken part of a Hermon Bar into the pot. It was creamy delicious.

"Everyone warmed up?" she asked them. "The sun will soon come around the mountain and reach this ridge. It's time for us to start before it gets too warm. The way to the top has few trees, so it's very exposed."

They started across the meadow toward the mountain. The path sometimes passed through groups of trees—not the tall pillars of the valley, but short and twisted trunks and branches. Soon the trail disappeared among the rock shelves and boulders that made up the broad ridge of the mountain.

"Time to bring out your compass, Maddie," instructed Rahab.

Maddie took off her pack and found the compass. "You'll have to show me how to use it, Rahab. I don't have a clue." Her cabin leader took out the map and showed them how to plot a route from where they stood, up along the ridge and to the peak.

"In some places ahead, as the ridge gets steeper, we won't see the top of the mountain. We will use the compass to make sure we stay on our route." Rahab adjusted the compass to point in the right direction. "It's an excellent lesson for life too. We can't always see where we are going. What—or who—helps you find your way?"

"My mom!" said Mia.

"The Bible, I guess," offered Ava.

"I know you want us to say 'Jesus,' " Rylie replied.

"Leaders, like you!" said Maddie.

"All true," Rahab agreed. "But Maddie, what if I'm not here? Who will lead them then?" She looked intently at Maddie, who didn't reply. After a moment, Rahab called out, "Okay, who wants to be the first to use the compass?"

Rylie took the first turn. She looked ahead at where the compass pointed and found a landmark, like a large boulder or a patch of flowers. Then she led the group to that spot and looked for the next landmark. Mia kept crying out, "There's the top of the mountain!" but it always turned out to be just another bump on the ridge. Ava tried the compass next, and then Maddie had a turn.

She picked out a finger of rock on the mountainside above them. The ridge was getting steeper now, and they sometimes had to use their hands as well as their feet to navigate it. As they came over the rise where the rock stood, they all gasped. Ahead of them stretched a broad patch of snow. They could see what was clearly the top of the mountain, still some distance above them. Which meant they would have to cross the snowfield!

The girls looked at each other and dove for the snow. With screams and laughter, snowballs flew and snow angels appeared. The melting snow soon soaked them, but the sun was now high and warm. They hung wet stuff to dry and pulled out crunchy crackers and cream cheese for lunch. And of course, Hermon Bars.

"Drink plenty of water today, girls," Rahab said. "We'll find many little streams to fill your water bottles again." She gave them a tablet to drop in their bottles to make sure the water was safe.

"How come some of the snow is pink?" Ava asked. "Is that why the mountain looked pink last night?"

"No, the setting sun turned the mountain pink," Rahab answered. "Green algae—a tiny plant—makes the snow pink."

"How come the snow isn't green then?" Ava protested.

"The algae defend themselves from the intense alpine UV rays by turning pink. Isn't that amazing?"

Rahab replied. "Which reminds me—it's time to reapply our sunscreen. With the higher altitude and the reflection off the snow, this sun can fry your fair skin."

"You and Rylie don't have to worry!" said Maddie.

"Even people with darker skin can get a sunburn up here," Rahab laughed. "But not as quickly as you." She scooped up a handful of pink snow. "This stuff is actually good for your skin. But don't eat any of it or you'll be running for the nearest cover with a roll of toilet paper!"

It was hard to move again after lunch. At first, it was fun to walk over the snowfield. But the snow was soft, and they were soon out of breath. Rahab was nearly at the top of the snowfield when they heard a scream. Ava had fallen and was sliding down the snowy slope on top of her backpack!

CAMP LIVERWURST & THE STRAY COMPASS

10. The Great Divide

"Stay where you are, girls!" Rahab dropped her pack and went whizzing down the slope on her boots after Ava. Thankfully, the snow leveled off at the bottom, so Ava stopped before she reached the rocks. But she must have been plenty scared because they saw her crying on Rahab's shoulder for several minutes. Rahab lifted Ava's backpack, and the two trudged back up to the rest of the group.

"Are you okay, Ava?" they all asked at once.

"Y-y-yeah," she replied. "It scared me because I was sliding down a mountain and couldn't see where I was going!"

"Which is an important lesson," said Rahab. "We crossed this snowfield only because it wasn't steep and it didn't end in a drop-off at the bottom. Snow and ice can be dangerous in the mountains."

"Shouldn't we be using our spiky shoe things?" asked Maddie.

"In some places, we will need them," Rahab replied. "But they're hard to walk in and not much help in soft snow. Come, let's keep moving. We need to reach the top and travel a distance down the other side before we stop tonight."

After the snowfield, they came to a place where a section of white rock—like giant stairs—rose steeply above them. The steps felt satisfyingly solid after the snow but were twice the height of stairs in a house. With their heavy packs on, the girls' legs soon became like rubber. Halfway up, they stopped and sat down on the steps.

"Ooohhhh!!!" they all said as they took in the view below them. "How can it possibly keep getting better?" Maddie exclaimed. The lake was a thin blue ribbon. They could see the river and the beach where the other girls were still waiting. All those tall forests were a fringe of dark green, highlighted by the brighter green of the meadows. The snowfield was blindingly white. And beyond were waves of mountain after mountain, and valley after valley, as far as the eye could see.

"We're nearly there, girls!" Rahab peeled them away from the view. The campers groaned their way up the rest of the steps. "We have one tricky section before we reach the summit." Maddie felt nervous when Rahab explained what they would need to do. But she trusted her cabin leader more and more with each step.

Above them, snow covered the final ridge on one side, and the other side was bare rock. The far edge of the snow looked as sharp as a knife. Rahab explained that this was a cornice, a snowbank formed by strong winter winds. It looked like you could walk right to the edge. But Rahab warned them that a cornice was like an overhanging wave of snow. It could break off and take a person with it into the deep valley below.

They kept to the rock at the closer edge of the snow. They could clearly see the top of the mountain above them now. But ahead, a band of snow intersected the rocky side of the ridge. They had no choice but to cross this steep snowfield.

"Time to put on your traction slippers—oh, that was an oxymoron!" laughed Rahab. "This is one of the trickier parts of our journey. You'll need your climbing harnesses too." She took a coil of climbing rope from her pack. The traction devices really were like slippers, but you wouldn't wear them in your house. These had lots of metal spikes to grip the hard snow and ice.

When the girls were ready, Rahab chose Maddie to go first. "You have the most experience at the climbing gym. I will belay you across, and the girls will clip in and follow you. Once they're across, you can belay me."

Rahab showed Maddie how to screw ice anchors into the snow along her route and clip the rope into them. The snow was hard and icy, but her spikes kept her from slipping. She could see that if someone crossed this section with no rope and no traction, it would be risky. A person wouldn't want to slide down this slope.

Maddie screwed in her last anchor and found a big rock to set her feet against. One by one, the girls followed while attached to the rope, and last came Rahab while Maddie belayed her. "Awesome, Maddie!" everyone said. "You did that like a pro!" It felt pretty good.

"This is it, girls!" Rahab called. "The summit is one more scramble up the rocks. Who will lead the way?"

"I will!" Rylie volunteered. "Who has the compass?"

"What do you need the compass for?" Maddie asked. "We can see the top from here!" She checked her pocket. "Where is the compass, anyway?" No one knew, and no one could remember who had used it last. "I'm pretty sure it wasn't me." Maddie looked around at the girls. "One of you must have it!" Everyone checked their pockets and packs, but the compass didn't show up.

As they followed Rylie toward the summit, Maddie was upset. Not only did she feel responsible for losing the compass, but it was precious to her because it was a gift. Rahab had called Maddie a compass, someone who would help other people find their way. And now the compass was gone. It gave her a hollow feeling inside.

"This is the top! I made it!" Rylie called out. She was standing on a big rock, and the others were soon beside her. All around, the view fell away beneath them, with more mountains and forests than Maddie thought possible. It felt incredible to make it to the summit of Mt. Hermon, which had seemed so far above them only yesterday. Everyone yelled and did a victory dance on the rock.

Everyone except Rahab. She stood still, gazing at the sky on the far side of the mountain. Maddie stopped and joined her. Huge black and purple clouds billowed in that direction. Below them, pillars of heavy rain hid the hills and forests. As Maddie watched, lightning flashed in the distance. Not long after, everyone heard the low grumble of thunder.

"Girls!" shouted Rahab. "Sorry to pull the plug on your party, but we need to get off the mountain, *now*! There's no time to lose!" The girls scrambled off the rock and grabbed their backpacks. Rahab gazed down another ridge. "I'm pretty sure this is the route, but I wish we still had the compass." Her words made Maddie's heart drop. The girls followed close behind their cabin leader. She led them down a slope like the one they had come up, but with no snow.

The wind gusted so suddenly, it nearly knocked the campers off their feet. Rahab took them to the side of the ridge where the wind was less, but the howling of the storm made Maddie anxious. The route down the ridge was easier than the one they came up. Maddie wondered why Rahab had thought this trail was more difficult. Then the group came to a stop. Below them was another section of snow that went right across the ridge. It was not wide, but very steep.

"We will need to rope up again, girls," Rahab explained. She gathered them into the shelter of an enormous boulder and looked at their scared faces. "I know you're afraid. I am too! When I'm afraid, I've learned to pray and put my trust in God, who has always been there for me, even when it didn't feel like it."

"When you trust him, are you not afraid anymore?" Ava asked anxiously.

"Oh, I'm still afraid!" Rahab admitted. "But when I talk with him and trust him, I also feel hope and confidence inside. I know that whatever happens, God's got this! Knowing he's there gives me the courage to face my fear."

"Well, let's talk with him, then!" Ava said, her voice trembling. "Now would be a good time."

Rahab raised her face against the wind and the clouds and prayed, "Father in heaven, here we are, in a storm on a mountain. I'm thankful for this big rock to huddle behind because it reminds us that you are our Rock and our Shelter. We ask you to protect us from the storm and bring us to a safe camping spot. We place ourselves in your kind and capable hands, in the name of Jesus! Amen."

Maddie was still afraid, but she felt some of what Rahab was talking about. She remembered what happened last summer when her friend Jayden was in a bad spot and he prayed. She hoped that the flicker of hope she felt inside was enough.

Rahab set up the rope like the last time, with Maddie leading. "We will make one change, Maddie. This time, when you get to the other side, I want you to unclip the rope and anchor it to something solid— a big rock will do. I'll do the same. I feel it will be safer this way." After crossing the snowfield, Maddie unclipped the rope from herself. She tied it around a large boulder, using the knots she knew from the climbing gym. Then Maddie found a good place to watch the others cross.

The sky was now dark with clouds, and the wind was cold. Thunder echoed constantly through the mountains. Maddie noticed that her hair felt like it did when she rubbed a balloon on her head—all prickly and staticky. Rylie clipped in first and crossed over to Maddie, followed by Mia. But something was wrong with Ava. She wouldn't clip in and instead clung to Rahab like she would never let go. Maddie thought she must be panicking because of the wild weather and steep slope. She was about to shout some encouragement when the unbelievable happened.

There was a brilliant flash of light, and at the same moment, a deafening boom. Lightning had struck the mountaintop exactly where they had been shortly before. It shook the rocks beneath their feet. With a grind and a roar, the snowfield between them broke away and disappeared over the edge, taking rocks and rope and ice screws with it. The three girls on one side and Ava and Rahab on the other stared across at one another in horror. Between them, there was now a sheer and impassible cliff.

CAMP LIVERWURST & THE STRAY COMPASS

11. Trusting Her Gut

Maddie's heart was pounding so hard, she was sure the others could hear it above the fading sound of thunder. Rahab shouted across the gap between them, "Maddie, keep going! Take the others down the mountain and find the trail back to camp. Before it gets dark, stop and make the best shelter you can!"

"What about you and Ava?" Maddie screamed back over the wind.

"Don't worry about us!" Rahab shouted. "We will return to the beach and wait with the others!"

"But the mountain and the lightning and… and the rope is gone…" Maddie protested.

"It's the only thing we can do, Maddie!" Rahab called. "Be strong now and very courageous! You are the leader—do you hear that, Rylie and Mia? Follow Maddie's lead."

"But Rahab, I don't know if I can…"

"Maddie, we need to go now!" Rahab interrupted. "It's okay, Maddie! I believe you were designed for this! God has prepared you for this very moment. I believe in the person he has made you!" She turned Ava around and quickly led her back toward the summit without another word.

For a moment, Maddie was stunned. Rylie and Mia stood with mouths open. Then something kicked in, and Maddie took charge. "Right! Packs on, girls! Let's get off this mountain!" Mia and Rylie looked doubtful. But they grabbed their backpacks and followed Maddie down the ridge without saying a word.

As confident as she sounded, Maddie was terrified. Rahab had not been sure that this was the correct ridge to follow, and they had no map or compass to guide them. What if they couldn't find the trail back to the camp? Relax, Maddie told herself. You *are* a compass! Someone who helps other people find their way. Trust your gut and you'll be fine.

They could still hear the roar of the wind on the ridge. The side of the mountain where Rahab had taken them was more sheltered. But they kept coming to places that were too steep to navigate. The only way they could keep going was to move closer to the top of the ridge. Soon, they were back in the full fury of the wind, which threatened to blow them right off the mountain.

And then the rain started.

This rain didn't fall down; it blew sideways, and sometimes even up as it streamed over the ridge. The girls ran for the shelter of a boulder that was the size of a whale and crouched down beside it. The wind was less, but the rain still swirled around them. Maddie remembered there was a part of a tent in her pack. She found the roll of nylon fabric and opened it up. The girls pulled the sheet over themselves and tucked in the edges that were being tugged by the wind.

"We need to wait for the storm to pass," Maddie told Mia and Rylie. "No use trying to walk through this. We might go over an edge!"

"I'm scared," said Mia.

"And cold!" said Rylie.

"We'll warm each other up," Maddie assured them. "Here, find a more comfortable spot. You can lean your heads on my shoulders." The girls huddled together with Maddie in the middle. For a long time, no one said anything. Maddie thought Mia might have gone to sleep. At least they were warm and mostly dry. But how long would the storm last?

"Maddie," began Rylie in a quiet voice, "I'm sorry we haven't been friends."

"Me too," said Maddie. Again, they were quiet for a while, until Maddie was sure she was the only one still awake. I must not sleep, she said to herself. I'm the leader! But she was warm and comfortable now. For the first time since leaving the top of the mountain, she felt safe. She thought about the girls on the beach and wondered if Rahab and Ava would make it back before dark or if they would have to camp out. She thought about unicorns, and Jayden and Evan riding them, and then… she didn't think about anything for a while.

Maddie woke with a start. The first thing she noticed was that it was quiet. She could hear the sleeping girls take turns breathing. Maddie pulled the nylon sheet off her head and looked out. The sunlight was warm and blinding, and the sky held only a few fluffy clouds. But the light was golden, and the sun was low in the sky. They had slept away the afternoon.

"Rylie! Mia!" she said gently. "Time to wake up! We need to get moving again!" Mia yawned and stretched, nearly punching Maddie in the nose. Rylie mumbled something about just another minute. Mia stood up and knocked the covering right off the three of them. Maddie could see across to the ridge where they had climbed the mountain. She could also see all the way down the ridge they were on to where the rocks ended and the meadow and forest started. This must be the right way to the camp! After all, she was the compass.

The way down the ridge was not difficult. But Mia seemed to have problems. She stumbled a lot and sometimes looked like she was in pain. Whenever Maddie asked, Mia said she was fine. The sun lingered just above the mountains across the lake when they reached the first of the alpine meadows. The flowers and tall grass were lit up so they could see every detail. But when the sun set, the sky grew dark quickly. By the time the girls reached the first of the trees, they could hardly see one another.

Maddie dug in her backpack for her flashlight. Rylie had a headlamp. Between them, they found a dry circle of fallen needles under a single fir tree. The girls collapsed on the soft bed of needles, exhausted. Mia curled up in a ball on the ground, whimpering. Maddie pulled out Mia's sleeping bag and helped her crawl inside.

After a few minutes, Maddie remembered she had part of the tent in her pack and pulled it out. "This doesn't look like a tent," she observed. "I think it's the piece that goes over the tent to keep the rain off. It will have to do." She tied one corner to the tree as high as she could reach and spread out the rest, anchoring the edges with rocks. It made for a cozy shelter. They had lots of room for their sleeping bags and packs.

"What about dinner?" asked Rylie.

"I don't know," Maddie replied, reaching into her pack. "What food do you have in your bag?"

Rylie searched and found a bag of bowl-sized discs. "Hermon Bars. How about you?"

Maddie pulled out a bag too and giggled, "More Hermon Bars! What about Mia?" She looked in Mia's backpack and found two cans of spaghetti sauce with meatballs. "Anyone have a can opener?" she asked. No one did. "Okay, Hermon Bars for dinner! Do you want fries with that?" Maddie and Rylie laughed.

Mia lay quietly in her sleeping bag, and Maddie wondered if she had gone back to sleep. But when they had her sit up for their Hermon Bar dinner, they could see she had been crying. "Mia, what's wrong?" Maddie asked.

"Oh Maddie," Mia moaned, "my feet hurt so bad!"

Carefully, they helped Mia take off her socks. Maddie gasped. Several places on Mia's heels and toes were red and raw with broken blisters. It looked so painful, Maddie wanted to cry. "Mia, why didn't you tell us?"

"I… I didn't want to look like a wimp," Mia sniffed. "And I didn't want Rahab to have to stop and fix my feet because she was in such a hurry." She winced as she wriggled her toes. "And now Rahab isn't here to help, and I don't know…" She started to cry again. Maddie gave her a hug, but her mind was whirling. She didn't know what to do either. How could they expect Mia to walk a step farther with feet like that?

"Maybe we should start a campfire and dry out her feet," Rylie suggested.

"Please!" said Mia. "I love campfires. I think it would help."

"But where will we find dry wood after all the rain?" Maddie asked. "Everything's soaked."

"Leave it to me," Rylie answered. "My mom showed me." She left the tent, and they heard her breaking branches from their tree. Maddie stepped out to join her. Rylie was piling up some of the broken branches on a flat rock near their shelter.

"These little branches are still dry, plus they're full of oils." Rylie lit her pile with a lighter, and it flared up quickly. "We'll need more. See what you can find, Maddie." She handed Maddie her headlamp. Maddie found lots of dry branches in the nearby forest and brought them back until they had a huge pile. Rylie kept snapping them and throwing them onto the fire. It grew into a warm blaze.

Maddie helped Mia outside and found a rock for her to sit on by the fire. The last colors of the sunset left the sky. As they munched on their Herman Bars, the girls watched the stars appear. "Not bad, for a bunch of kids," said Rylie.

When their pile of wood ran out, they decided to go to bed and make an early start, hoping Mia's feet were better. But Maddie had her doubts and wondered what to do if Mia couldn't walk in the morning. It took her a long time to get to sleep, and when she did, she had a vivid dream.

Maddie dreamed she was looking for the trail to the camp but could find no sign of it. She glanced up and saw Rahab sitting on a boulder, watching her. "Are you really here?" Maddie asked hopefully.

"No, it's just a dream," Rahab laughed. "See? I'll prove it!" She transformed into a purple unicorn with a horn of solid gold. "What do you think?" it said.

"That's cool," said Maddie, "but I like you better as Rahab."

And suddenly, there was Rahab again. "Maddie, why can't you find your way?"

Maddie frowned. "I guess I'm not a good compass after all."

"Maddie, when I said you were a compass, I didn't mean you should trust in your own ability to help others find their way."

"What do you mean?" Maddie asked.

"Well, a compass doesn't have inside it everything needed to point out the right direction," Rahab explained. "It has to reach outside itself to something a whole lot bigger."

"The magnetic North Pole!" Maddie exclaimed. "I remember from science class."

"So, Maddie, what is outside of you, is way bigger than you, and will help you find your way?" As Rahab said this, she became a purple unicorn again, sprouted wings and flew away.

But when Maddie woke up early the next morning, she couldn't remember her dream, as hard as she tried.

12. Hopelessly Stuck

The crows woke Maddie, Mia and Rylie in the morning. It sounded like a hundred of them in their tree, all cawing at the same time. Maddie held her hands over her ears, but it was no use. She left her sleeping bag and went yelling around the tree until every crow flew away.

Maddie looked around her. The sun had not yet come up over the far ridge of the mountain, so it was pretty cold. She sat on a rock with her sleeping bag pulled up over her head. But she had no Rahab, and no cup of hot chocolate to warm her hands. She wondered if she could lead the girls back to Camp Liverwurst that day and sleep in a proper bed. She sure hoped so.

Rylie came out of the shelter and began breaking more branches for a fire. Maddie was about to tell her not to bother since they would need to leave soon, but she didn't want to sound bossy. Rylie was great at building campfires. She soon had one crackling merrily.

"I'll see if I can find the start of the trail back to camp, okay?" Maddie told Rylie. "Stay with Mia, please. She would freak out if she woke up and we were both gone." Rylie nodded, but didn't say anything and kept tossing sticks in the fire.

Maddie wandered along the edge of the forest, looking for the trail. A few places looked like paths, but when she tried them, they quickly dwindled away. She continued until she had left the ridge and started to descend into a valley. Maddie turned around and retraced her steps, seeking any sign that people had walked this way. There was nothing.

"Maybe this wasn't the right ridge after all," she said to herself. She looked up toward the mountain and saw the ridge they had come down. To one side, she saw the ridge where they had climbed up. But she also saw another ridge on the other side. It looked steep and had lots of patches of snow. Could that be the ridge leading to the trail? And if it was, how could they reach it now? A deep, forested valley lay between her and that ridge.

She heard a snap behind her and whirled around. To her relief, it was Rylie. She was looking at something in her hand, which she abruptly put in her pocket. "Rylie!" Maddie exclaimed. "You were supposed to stay with Mia!"

"She's already up," Rylie snapped. "I was getting bored, so I came to find you and collect more branches." Maddie didn't like her answer. She didn't think it was a good idea for Mia to be alone, and said so. Rylie answered, "Who made you the boss?"

"Rahab did. Remember?" Maddie felt her bad temper rising. "She told you to follow my lead."

"Yeah, but she didn't say I have to do everything you tell me to!" Rylie answered.

The two girls glared at one another for a moment. Maddie knew it would be easy to erupt and say a bunch of stuff she would later regret. Angry words sparked up in her brain, but she didn't let them catch hold. They sputtered and died out. What would Rahab do in this situation? She had been so patient with Maddie, even when it couldn't have been easy.

Maddie sighed and let her tense shoulders slump. "Here, let me help you find more branches, Rylie." The girls searched for branches under the eaves of the forest and soon had more than they could carry.

"Did you find the trail, Maddie?" Rylie asked.

"No," Maddie replied. "I looked carefully all along the edge of the forest. The trail isn't here."

"I didn't think so. I was just…" Rylie hesitated.

"Just what?"

"Nothing," Rylie replied hastily. "But I'm pretty sure we took the wrong ridge down the mountain. Remember Rahab saying the route was challenging? Except for the snowfield, the ridge we took down was easier than the one we took up."

"I was thinking the same thing," said Maddie. "You're pretty good at outdoor stuff, Rylie. That was a great fire we had last night."

"Um, thanks!" Rylie replied. They looked at one another, and they were no longer glaring. But Rylie seemed uncomfortable and soon turned away.

Just then, they heard a loud crackling sound in the direction of their shelter. The girls jumped up and sprinted to see what was happening. As they ran, they saw a huge plume of smoke billowing straight up in the sky. "Mia!" Maddie yelled. "Are you okay?"

When they arrived at their campsite, Mia was standing in her bare feet. Her hands were over her mouth as she watched their tree burn like a giant torch. Roaring flames leaped above the tree. A towering column of dark gray smoke climbed into the sky. "Get back, Mia!" Maddie yelled. She grabbed Mia around the middle and carried her a safe distance from the tree. Even there, they could feel the heat.

"Are you okay, Mia?" Maddie asked, looking her over. "Were you burned anywhere?" Mia shook her head and burst into tears.

It took a while before she could tell them what had happened. "I was… I was… just playing with sticks in the campfire. And the needles caught fire, and I tried…" And she started crying again.

The fire didn't last long. The tree was now a smoking black skeleton of trunk and branches. Sparks and glowing bits of wood fell to the ground. Maddie was glad the next nearest trees were far enough away that they didn't catch fire too. The column of smoke still hung high in the sky. Maddie made the girls stay back and wait for everything to cool down. They could see that their shelter was half gone, and their packs were scorched.

"Whoa!" Rylie breathed. "That was awesome—and terrifying!"

Maddie didn't know what to say. Everything kept getting worse and worse! No cabin leader, no trail and now no shelter. They had to reach the camp today! She took a few steps toward the tree, but everything was still too hot. Should they wait to collect their stuff or leave now? Then she remembered Mia, who was barefoot and clinging to Rylie, trembling.

Maddie gently led Mia to a nearby rock. Mia winced at every step. "Let's look at your feet, Mia," Maddie offered. The girl's feet didn't look as raw but were still very red and sore. "Where are your socks and boots, Mia?" she asked. Mia pointed to the tree, and Maddie could see two misshapen lumps that could have once been Mia's boots. Maddie sighed. This was it, then. Mia wasn't going anywhere without a ride. And they couldn't carry her even if they knew where they were going.

"What will we do now?" asked Rylie.

Maddie didn't answer. She didn't have an answer. Why should she know what to do? She was just a kid too! Maddie didn't like everyone expecting her to give them directions. But Rahab made her the leader. What's more, she called her a compass…

Maddie gasped. An image came to her from her dream. Rahab, sitting on a boulder. Maddie said to the girls, "I'll be back in a minute! Stay here—like, really stay this time, Rylie!" She walked along the tree line as she had earlier that morning. The sun was now in her eyes, warming her all over. When she came to a large boulder, Maddie almost expected to see Rahab sitting on it. But of course, she wasn't.

What had Rahab said to her in the dream? Something about being a compass. Maddie closed her eyes to the sun and imagined the needle of a compass. It swung back and forth in smaller and smaller sweeps until it pointed… North! That was it! The magnetic

North Pole! The compass required more than what was inside it to point out the right direction. It needed something… outside itself… big… making it able to show the way.

Maddie went down on her knees and lifted her arms like Rahab did when she prayed. "God, I thought it was up to me to find the way back to camp. But I can't!" She told Jesus how the snowfield collapsed and about losing their leader. Maddie explained about going down the wrong ridge and finding no trail. She mentioned Mia's sore feet and burned-up boots. "Everything has gone wrong, and I know I don't have enough in me to get us back to camp. God, I'm only a compass! Please point me in the right direction!"

She cried a little, and it felt good to let go of the emotions bottled up inside. She felt more at peace, knowing that not everything was up to her. Maddie had no idea what God would do about their helpless situation, but she felt okay about that. It was like Priscilla said: Jesus gave her the strength to be content and thankful, even when everything had gone wrong. She knelt until her knees became sore, then stood and walked back to the others to wait and see what would happen. She could do nothing else.

Rylie and Mia were playing a clapping game together when Maddie returned. She was glad to see that Rylie stayed put and found a way to keep Mia's mind off her painful feet. Mia and Rylie stopped their game and glanced up at her. Then they gasped. The girls stared with open mouths and wide eyes at something right behind Maddie.

13. The Unexpected Visitors

What in the world were Mia and Rylie staring at? Maddie turned around.

Standing by the burnt tree and stamping their hooves were two unicorns. They were as white as the snow on the mountains behind them. Sitting astride the unicorns—with shocked expressions to match the look on the girls' faces—were two boys. They were Evan and Jayden.

Rylie broke the stunned silence first. "What in the world are you doing here?" she shouted. "And what on Earth are you riding?" she asked in wonder. Maddie realized that her cabinmates had not yet seen the unicorns. Rylie took a step toward them, stopped and put her hands on her hips. "Are you real?"

"Yeah, we're real!" Evan laughed. "But where are we? And what are you doing here? And what's with this burnt matchstick of a tree?"

Maddie finally got her voice back. "Oh wow, am I ever glad to see you! But how…" She motioned at the unicorns, at a loss for words again.

"Why don't we sit down and figure this out," suggested Jayden, dismounting from his unicorn. The campers sat in a circle on the ground. One unicorn laid down with its back against Maddie's and promptly went to sleep. "Yeah, they do that around girls," said Jayden. "Noah says that the same thing happens in all the old stories about unicorns."

Maddie briefly told the boys about their journey—the capsized boat, the mountain, the storm and the avalanche, Mia's sore feet and the torched tree. She didn't mention her dream about Rahab. "And now we can't find the trail back to the camp. Even if we could, Mia can't walk."

Evan explained about the unicorns. "We've been riding them everywhere around the camp—so fun! But we were warned by... someone-we-all-love-who-has-a-beard-and-lots-of-animals... that strange things can happen when you ride a unicorn."

"How come you didn't say No-...?" Rylie started to say. The unicorn behind Maddie snorted and raised its head.

Evan cut her off. "Stop! Don't say his name, whatever you do! I'll explain." He looked frightened for a moment but sighed in relief. "You see, unicorns are spacetime travelers."

"You mean like in Back to the Future?" asked Mia.

"Well, kind of," replied Evan. "But they not only travel through time; they also travel through space. It means they can show up anywhere and anytime, in an instant. That's how... the-guy-who's-name-I-can't-say... got the unicorns to Camp Liverwurst. He traveled with them from another time and another place."

"Yeah, but you can't make unicorns take you where and when you want," Jayden explained. "They will go if they want to and if they have a good reason to go. So… that man… warned us that when we were riding them, we could suddenly find ourselves… well… anywheretime! Any place and any time."

"But why can't you say the name 'No-' " Mia started.

"Mia!" everyone else shouted at the same time. Mia withered and put her hands over her mouth. The unicorns shook their heads anxiously.

"Because," explained Evan, "that-guy told us that wherewhenever the unicorns took us, we could always return to him immediately by saying his name. If you said his name right now, the unicorns would disappear and we would all be stuck!"

"Yikes!" said Maddie. "But we still don't know why and how you ended up here."

"We don't know either," said Jayden. "We were riding across the playing field by the bike shed. We noticed a column of smoke rising near one of the mountains. Everyone had seen the lightning storm up there the day before. We had decided to go and tell… uh, the-guy …about a possible forest fire on the mountain, when WHOOSH! We found ourselves here!"

"I guess the unicorns were curious about the fire," said Evan. "Good thing, too! It seems you're in a bit of a pickle."

"Can you take us all back on the unicorns?" asked Rylie.

"I don't know," Evan answered. "I guess we can try." He called his unicorn and mounted it. "See if it will take Mia too," he suggested. But as soon as they tried to lift Mia onto its back, the unicorn shied away. Evan dismounted, and they tried Mia again. The unicorn let her mount this time. But within a minute, the animal sagged to its knees, put its head down and went to sleep.

"I guess we should have expected that!" laughed Evan. "But it looks like the unicorns will only take one rider at a time. And we don't know if we can convince the unicorns to make a second trip to this place. Mia needs to go, for sure. We'll have to be quick before the unicorn falls asleep under her. But who else should go?"

"You should," replied Jayden. "I'll stay and help Maddie and Rylie find the trail back to camp."

"And don't forget to send a rescue party to pick up the girls and leaders at the beach," Maddie reminded them. She was a bit disappointed that it was Jayden, not Evan, who would hike back with them. And envious that Mia got to ride the spacetime-traveling unicorn. But she shook it off and became the leader again. "Okay, you take Mia. We'll clean up this mess and find our way back as best we can."

Evan mounted his unicorn again. "See you soon! On the count of three, toss Mia onto the other unicorn and shout... that-guy's name. Ready? One, two..."

On three, they lifted Mia onto the unicorn, stood back and shouted, "NOAH!" At one moment, there were Evan and Mia and two unicorns. In less than the blink of an eye, Maddie, Rylie and Jayden stood alone by the burnt tree. Maddie gave her head a shake. She wondered if anything weirder could happen on their strange and unexpected journey.

The tree was now cool enough that they could clean up their shelter area. Not wanting to leave any junk behind, they stuffed the scorched shelter and Mia's roasted boots into the packs. The shoulder straps on one pack were half-melted, but Jayden took that one and did what he could to make it work. "I'm glad Mia's taken care of," he said, "but the unicorns didn't solve the problem of finding the trail back to camp. Do you have a compass?"

"We did, but we can't find it," Maddie answered. Rylie busied herself with rearranging her pack and didn't join the conversation. "Anyway, I'm not sure how it would help us without a map. Are you good at finding your way, Jayden?"

"Me?" he said in surprise. "I'm hopeless with directions. Sometimes I get lost in my own neighborhood! What do you think we should do?"

Maddie looked at Jayden and Rylie for a moment and said, "I want to tell you about my dream." She explained what Rahab told her about being a compass. Maddie admitted that she didn't have everything that was needed to find the way. "So I prayed and told God about the mess we were in, and not long after, you and Evan showed up!"

No one said anything for a moment. Jayden asked, "So if we pray again, will some other crazy thing like that happen?"

"I don't think so," Maddie replied. "I mean, the unicorns were a big deal, but they only solved one part of our problem. They were like the icing on the cake. But I couldn't guess in a hundred years what God will do now." Maddie stood up. "All we can do is ask him!"

"That works for me!" said Jayden, standing too. "I mean really, it did—last summer, when I was at camp and lost in the woods. But you're right, I could never have imagined how he would answer that time, either." He looked at Rylie. "Would you like to join us?" Rylie shook her head and stayed busy with her pack. Both Maddie and Jayden prayed and asked God to provide a way to return to camp. At the end, Maddie prayed, "Jesus, thank you for this adventure! I hope it teaches us to trust you more. Amen."

Even after putting on their packs, Maddie wasn't sure what to do. "This ridge is a dead end. We can't find our way to camp through these woods. We could try going back up this ridge, but I don't like the looks of the ridge next to it. We don't know if it's the right one either. But it seems that uphill is our only option."

It was harder than Maddie expected to walk up the ridge they had come down the day before. They had to stop often, and finally Rylie plunked herself down against a boulder. "I think my battery is dead," she complained.

"Did you have any breakfast?" Jayden asked. Rylie had finished her Hermon Bar and the rest of her water; Maddie hadn't eaten anything. They showed Jayden their useless cans of spaghetti sauce and meatballs. "Oh, that's no problem!" he said. "I saw a video about how to do this." He took a can and rubbed the top of it on a flat rock beside him. After a few minutes of this, he rinsed off the top with Maddie's water bottle. Then he squeezed the can, and the lid popped off!

It sounds gross, but anyone who has been hiking in the mountains for two days and has nothing left to eat will say the same as Maddie, Rylie and Jayden: cold spaghetti sauce with meatballs is awesome! They also filled up their water bottles from a tiny trickle of water that Rylie found, adding the tablets Rahab had given them to make the water safe.

Maddie was about to say how much better she felt. Suddenly, there was a loud swoosh and a blast of air directly over their heads. The girls screamed and dove to the ground. A gigantic bird landed on the boulder they were using as a dining room table, knocking the empty cans flying with a clatter.

14. Follow the Leader

The enormous bird startled Jayden too. But something like this had happened to him and Maddie once before, and he laughed. "Zesi! You could drop by without scaring us to death!" The creature folded its wings and stared eye-to-eye at Jayden. "Rylie, meet Zesi!" he said. "This is John's eagle. But according to John, you could just as well say he's her human." Jayden explained that John was one of the staff at the camp and that the eagle helped them in lots of ways.

Picking themselves up off the ground, the girls admired the eagle—from a safe distance. Maddie remembered that the bird had brought them a message the summer before. She wondered if that was why Zesi had come this time. Maddie looked at the curved yellow beak. Nothing there. She jumped back as Zesi beat her massive wings and made a loud "Crrrii-ii-ii-ii" sound, and then she saw it.

Rylie did too. "There's something attached to one of her legs," she shouted. Right above the eagle's long and sharp talons was a roll of paper fastened with red twine. How could they reach it without being sliced into ribbons? "I'm not touching that!" said Rylie.

Jayden wasn't eager to try either, which left Maddie. She gritted her teeth and reached under the bird's body. To her relief, Zesi extended a leg toward her and let her remove the roll.

"What's it say?" asked Rylie impatiently.

Maddie untied the paper and unrolled it. What on Earth? "All it says is, 'Follow the leader.' " She looked up at Jayden and Rylie. "What's that supposed to mean?"

"It's a reminder, I guess," said Jayden. "You're the leader, so we're supposed to follow you."

"Yeah, except I don't know where I'm going!" Maddie moaned. "This message isn't any help at all." No one had any ideas, so they sat and stared at the eagle, who was busy tugging loose bits of fluff from her shoulder. Then Maddie had a thought. "Hey, last time Zesi brought us a message, she didn't stick around long; she took off again right away. Why is she still here?" The eagle stared at her unblinking, as if she should know the answer.

"Maybe Zesi is the leader now," Rylie suggested.

At first, Maddie didn't like the idea of following a bird. Rahab had made Maddie the leader! But she didn't know the way, and obviously Zesi did. She also remembered Rahab saying that the best leader would be the one who was the best follower. Well, since she didn't know where to lead them at the moment, it might be time to follow.

"I think you're right, Rylie," Maddie agreed. "But how will Zesi lead us? Eagles don't walk!"

"Maybe we could say her handler's name, like we did with the unicorns," suggested Jayden. "But I suppose if we do, Zesi might fly back to him."

"I think that's the best suggestion yet," said Maddie. "And I'm not sure what else to do. We should give it a try. Let's pack up and see what happens."

When everyone was ready, Maddie gazed into the eagle's eyes and said, "Zesi, take us to John, please. John, Zesi!" Immediately, the eagle stretched out and lifted into the air. Maddie felt the wind from its wings. "No! She's going to fly away and leave us here!" Maddie cried.

But she didn't. Zesi soared a short distance up the ridge and landed on another boulder. She turned toward them and made her "Crrrii-ii-ii-ii" sound. "She wants us to follow!" Rylie shouted. "I knew it!" The campers scrambled to their feet and made their way toward the eagle. Before they reached her, Zesi took flight again and landed farther up the ridge. But she led them away from the side where they had come down the day before.

Today, the breeze was light and cool, which they appreciated because the sun was beating down on them. When they stopped to catch their breath, Maddie had everyone put on more sunscreen and have a good drink. Zesi perched a distance away, preening herself patiently until they were ready to move on. Now she was no longer taking them up the mountain, but across a wide slope toward the next ridge. Clusters of tiny wildflowers dotted the rocky mountainside.

They were following what appeared to be a trail made by animals, and Maddie wondered what they were. She soon found out. Jayden was ahead, and as he came to a corner, he suddenly crouched down and motioned for the others to be silent. They came up beside him, and on the mountainside they saw a small herd of white animals with short, black horns. "Mountain goats!" Rylie whispered excitedly. The mountain goats looked nervous about Zesi, perhaps because two of them were kids (not children, baby goats!). They soon fled up the mountain with enormous bounds.

"That was awesome," said Rylie. "I've only ever seen pictures of them before." Maddie and Jayden agreed. Zesi crrrii-ii-ii-ii-ed at them again, and they continued. They soon found themselves on the next ridge, right near the tree line. There, plain to see, was a trail leading down into the woods. Maddie was so relieved, she would have hugged Zesi if she dared. Instead, the eagle rose once more into the air, climbing in higher and higher circles until she was a dot in the sky.

Maddie, Rylie and Jayden were now hot and tired. They took shelter from the sun in a thicket of short fir trees and drank their water. Jayden dug around in the pack he was carrying. "What in the world is this?" he asked, holding up a misshapen brown disc.

"Hermon Bar!" Maddie and Rylie shouted together. Jayden was pretty impressed with how good the bar tasted as he shared it with the girls. "We're glad you found that, Jayden!" they said. "Best surprise ever!"

"I wish Zesi hadn't left us," Rylie said with her mouth full of Hermon Bar. "Do you think you can find the way back to camp now, Maddie?"

Maddie smiled at her. "Think about it, Rylie! We prayed, and look what happened. Two people show up on unicorns. Mia gets a safe ride back to camp. An eagle shows us the way to the trail and then takes off. Does that sound like an ordinary day to you?"

"I guess not," Rylie answered. "But what does it all mean?"

"It means Someone is taking care of us," explained Maddie. "We don't need Zesi to lead us anymore, or she would have stayed. Jesus is and always has been our leader."

"He's our Trailblazer," Jayden chipped in.

"He's a truck?" said Rylie with a smirk.

"You know what I mean," Jayden laughed. "Jesus will show us the way. He's been doing that all along."

Rylie looked thoughtful for a moment and reached into her pocket. She held out a small object to Maddie and said quietly, "Um, I'm the one who swiped the compass."

Maddie took the compass and opened it. She watched the needle swing slowly back and forth until it pointed right at her. She looked up at Rylie. "Thank you for telling me, Rylie," she said gently. "Would you like to tell me why you wanted the compass?"

Rylie picked up a small rock and stared at it, turning it over and over. "It's… it's not that I wanted the compass so badly, Maddie," she sniffed. "I wanted to be *you*! And when I saw that Rahab had given you the compass, I just had to have it. I thought it would make me feel like the leader instead of you. I'm sorry, Maddie!"

Rylie looked up at her hopefully, and any hard feelings in Maddie's heart melted away. She reached over and gave Rylie a huge hug. "It makes me feel good that you want to be like me," Maddie told her. "But I would rather get to know you as Rylie! Can we be friends?" Rylie hugged her back.

Maddie wondered what Jayden thought of all this girl stuff, but she saw he had a big smile on his face. "All good, then?" he asked brightly. "Because if you are, we might still have a long walk before we reach Camp Liverwurst!"

They set out again. The soft trail through the woods was refreshing after walking over hot rocks all day. The route wasn't difficult, but after several hours they were all wondering how far they still had to go. They saw only trees and path, with no viewpoints to give them any idea of where they were. "I don't know how much longer I can do this," panted Rylie. "Those cans of spaghetti sauce seem like a long time ago."

At least they came across plenty of streams to keep their water bottles full. One creek had an emerald green pool with a small waterfall flowing out of it. Rylie walked right into the water, boots and all, and sat down. She gritted her teeth and blew her breath out because it was icy cold. But when she came out, she said it made her feel better. Maddie and Jayden took her word for it.

The sun was now hidden by the trees. When the campers felt they couldn't take one more step, they heard a sound ahead of them. It was the clatter of hooves! Coming around a corner was Noah, riding a unicorn and leading another unicorn and two horses behind him.

"Well met!" Noah shouted. "I figured you might get tired and hungry on your epic journey, so I thought I would come and meet you!"

Maddie laughed. "Oh Noah, you have no idea how glad we are to see you! Can I stop being the leader now?"

"I'm afraid not." Noah dismounted, and Maddie gave him a hug. "It will not always be your turn to lead, Maddie, but I believe you will always have the heart of a leader."

Noah lifted a saddlebag from one of the horses. "First things first!" he exclaimed. "Let's find a place to sit and enjoy a meal together since we'll be late for dinner in the dining hall." He pulled out steaming containers of beef stew and a basket of warm, fresh-made biscuits. Nothing ever tasted better.

"Do we still have a long way to go, Noah?" asked Rylie as she buried a biscuit in butter and strawberry jam.

"Yes, it's still quite a distance. Our four-hooved friends will make the journey easier for you. But by the end, your bottoms might be as sore as your legs are right now!"

"Did someone pick up Rahab and Priscilla and the girls?" asked Maddie.

"Oh yes! By now, they're unpacked and showered, and more than ready for dinner. Well, as long as dinner is anything but Hermon Bars!"

"I could still eat another Hermon Bar," Rylie murmured.

"I guess you and Jayden will ride the unicorns," said Maddie wistfully, "and Rylie and I will have the horses." Noah didn't answer, but he had a twinkle in his eye.

15. Made For This

Rahab, Priscilla and their girls weaved through the crowd in a conga line, each person with their hands on the shoulders of the camper in front of them. Even Mia hobbled along in her bare feet. Miriam and David were singing one of the campers' favorites, the same song Rahab once sang with the rescue team:

Let's make some noise!
Joyful noise to our God!
Let's make some noise!
Sing and laugh out loud!
Because God is God (not us!)
He made us, we didn't make him

Ava, who was at the back of the line, felt a new set of hands on her shoulders. Who had joined their line? She turned her head to look. "Maddie!" she squealed. "It's Maddie and Rylie and... some guy!" The line of girls broke up into a confusion of hugs and cries of joy as they welcomed home their heroes. Even Jayden got his fair share of hugs, though most of the girls didn't know who he was.

The girls had a million questions for one another, but the answers would have to wait. As the music ended, the elderly Moses walked up to the front. He was not wearing his usual yellow clothes. Instead, he had on funny leather shorts, a plaid shirt, suspenders, a green peaked hat with a feather, and tall hiking boots. He was carrying a long, decorated walking stick. "Good evening, everyone," Moses began. "How do I look? Ready for a mountain adventure?" The campers cheered.

"I love climbing mountains! I have summited many mountains in my day, and I bet I could still keep up with most of you if we were to climb together. I want to tell you a story from my younger days, when I was hiking and saw a most extraordinary thing." Moses told them about finding a bush that was on fire but never burned up, and about the Voice that spoke to him out of the fire.

"I asked him his name. He said, 'I Am Who I Am.' I wished I had his kind of confidence! This was at a time in my life when I didn't know who I was anymore, or what I was doing out there in the wilderness. The Lord God said, 'I have a job for you.' I kept telling him I didn't think I was the guy he was looking for. But he wouldn't take 'no' for an answer. I ended up saying yes, and it changed my life. The rest is—quite literally—history!

"I'm telling you this because people will say that you can be anyone you want to be. I suppose that's true, though the idea has led many people to great disappointments. But what if God designed you with a purpose in mind? Wouldn't you want to know who you really are, and what he has prepared for you to accomplish in this world?

"I want you to know that you are God's work of genius, his… magnus opus, his… his… tour de force!" Moses was getting excited. "You are his invention. He knows who you are and what he designed you for in this world. And as you come to know your Maker, you will come to know yourself.

"Tonight, I want to introduce you to some extraordinary fellow hikers. Rahab, Maddie, Rylie and Mia, come up and join me. And you too, Jayden!" Maddie and Rylie looked at each other in surprise and made their way to the front with the others. "Here are some brave hikers who volunteered for a rescue mission on behalf of their cabinmates. In the last few days, they climbed the heights of Mt. Hermon, forded a river, crossed steep snowfields and walked long distances with little food.

"When Jayden had the opportunity to trade places with Mia, who was injured, he didn't hesitate," Moses continued. "You see, what God has in mind for you to do in this world is not in some distant future. It is today; it is every day. It's about your way of life. What has God designed you to do in the next half hour? Or the next time you have the chance to do someone a kindness?"

Moses continued talking for a while, forgetting that he had left Maddie and the others standing beside him. Maddie didn't mind. As she looked at the faces of the campers listening to Moses, she said to herself, This is who I am. I didn't know it, but God knew it all along. I am a compass. I point people to Jesus, and he shows us the way. If Maddie wants to know Maddie better,

Maddie has to get to know Jesus better. Ms. Williams was right, and now I know she was right.

As the last song finished, Maddie spotted her friend Olivia on the other side of the room, excitedly talking with the girls from her cabin. Maddie was glad. As much as she missed Olivia, she didn't want to get in the way of her time with those girls. She and Olivia were still best friends, and they would have loads to talk about when they arrived home. She followed Rahab and the others to the dining hall for the snack.

"But how were you able to ride the unicorns?" Lizzy asked at their table. Jayden and Evan had joined them too. "I thought you said the unicorn fell asleep under Mia!"

Maddie's heart swelled at the beautiful memory of riding the unicorn toward the setting sun earlier that evening. "Noah, of course. He told us that unicorns absolutely love stories. As long as we keep telling them a story while we're riding, the unicorns stay awake to find out what happens next."

"That must have been a long story!" Evan exclaimed.

"Maddie and I took turns picking up the story where the other left off," said Rylie. "It was kinda fun. But don't ask me what the story was about! There was a golden key and an island and a rhinoceros and— nope, that's all I've got!" The campers laughed.

"You were gone for such a long time!" said Chloe. "Priscilla made it really fun at the beach. But if I never eat another Hermon Bar in my life, I'm okay with that!"

Long before the girls stopped asking them questions, Maddie and Rylie started drooping. "Time to head to the cabin, girls," said Rahab. "It's been a long day, and we still have lots of camp left! I'm so glad to have us all back together again. And… I think I have one more Hermon Bar in my pack, if anyone…" The girls groaned, and then tackled her.

The last few days of camp went by far too fast. Maddie got to do all the things she was hoping for, but now with a new group of friends. Her cabin group rocked the night game and came in second place for the best-decorated cabin. Maddie helped Ava overcome her fear of heights in the climbing gym. Her cabin group played so much archery tag, no other cabin would challenge them anymore. And of course, she and Rylie rode the unicorns any chance they got. By the end, they were seriously running out of stories to tell them. But they never had the chance to do any spacetime traveling with the unicorns. That was okay—Camp Liverwurst was the place where Maddie wanted to be.

On the last night of camp, Maddie had another dream. When she woke up the next morning, she couldn't get it out of her mind. In her dream, she saw a boat like Rahab's dory, but with only one person in it. They had no oars, and the water spread to the horizon in every direction with no land in sight. She was crying because the person in the boat had nowhere to go, and no way of getting there even if they did. If only they had a compass and a pair of oars, they could find their way home, the place where they belonged.

She decided to ask Rahab about her dream. "Maddie, my guess is that you know someone who is like the person in the boat," suggested Rahab.

"Yeah, I wondered if it might be my dad," Maddie answered. Rahab asked why with a tilt of her head. "Because," Maddie continued, "my dad believes there's only us in the universe. He thinks our only purpose is to go on existing as long and as well as we can. It's like being in the boat in my dream. There's no purpose and nowhere to go; he's drifting in an endless ocean. And then there's me, and I'm a compass. I was wondering if I could point out the right way to him, and how."

"Yes, I think you will, Maddie," Rahab answered. "Most of the time, it will simply mean being Maddie in your home. Your dad may not always want to hear about Jesus. But he won't be able to ignore Jesus showing up in the way you live your life. I think he will soon become curious about the hope and sense of direction you have. I believe you will get to be a compass to him."

The last morning of camp arrived like an unexpected unicorn. Maddie couldn't believe how fast the week had gone. They were on the dock, ready to board Noah's ferry (since Rahab's boat hadn't been recovered yet). Maddie said to Rylie, "I want you to have this." She handed Rylie the compass. "It's to help you remember me. I hope that whenever you use it, you'll remember that you have a friend who is a compass."

Tears formed in Rylie's eyes. She reached over and gave Maddie a hug and whispered, "I'll never forget you, Maddie!" They turned their unicorns up the gangplank, telling them stories all the way.

Recipe for Hermon Bars

(Get permission and help from a parent/guardian!)

Ingredients:

- Dried fruit – 250 ml / 1 cup
- Nuts and seeds – 250 ml / 1 cup (ones you and your family and friends aren't allergic to)
- Chocolate chips or wafers – 500 g / 1 pound

1. Put all ingredients in a leaky plastic bag, go out in a boat and capsize (make sure it's summer and you're wearing a floatation device).
2. Get to shore and spread ingredients on a large tarp to dry.
3. [Alternatively, you can skip the whole boat adventure and put all the ingredients in a medium microwavable bowl.]
4. Heat the mixture in the microwave for 30 seconds, remove and stir. Then keep heating it further for 15 seconds at a time, stirring each time, until it looks like cake batter. Be sure not to put a metal spoon in the microwave, and don't overheat!
5. Scoop mixture into plastic bowls or small containers (careful, it's very hot!). Or, make mini-bars in an ice cube tray. Allow them to cool completely.
6. When fully cool, pop your Hermon Bars out of their bowls and enjoy!

Discussion Questions

If you are a camper, this section will help you think about each chapter. The goal is to decide what you will do about what you are learning.

If you are a cabin leader, you can use these questions and activities as a guide (not a script!) for discussion to help campers process the chapters you read to them. Plan on reading two to three chapters per day—for cabin devotions, during wake-up, after a meal or on a break.

Each set of questions has three parts:
1. **Ready** – Questions or an activity to help campers get ready to discuss God's word with you.
2. **Set** – Questions to set in their minds the big idea of a Bible passage (see the headings for each chapter below).
3. **Go** – Questions or an activity to help them decide what to do about what they learned.

Chapter 1 – God gives generously to people who ask.
1. **Ready** – When did you start packing for camp? Is there anything you left behind?
2. **Set** – James 1:5-6 – Have you ever felt like a wave, tossed back and forth? How did wisdom help you in that situation? How did you get it?
3. **Go** – If God was sitting on the bunk next to you, and you could ask him one question, what would it be?

Chapter 2 – Thanking God is trusting God.

1. **Ready** – Tell us about a time when you were disappointed that things didn't turn out as you expected.

2. **Set** – 1 Thessalonians 5:16-18 – What is God's will for you? Why do you think God wants us to rejoice, pray and be thankful in every circumstance?

3. **Go** – Tell us two things you are thankful for and one thing that's hard to be thankful for.

Chapter 3 – Love overlooks many kinds of wrongs.

1. **Ready** – *Pass around a bowl of pebbles. Each camper takes as many or as few as they want.* For each pebble you took, tell something about yourself.

2. **Set** – 1 Peter 4:8-9 – Tell us an example of how love could "cover over" an unloving thing people might do or say to one another.

3. **Go** – Look around the room and—without telling—choose one person that you will try to be a friend to tomorrow.

Chapter 4 – Jesus gives us the strength to be content.

1. **Ready** – Finish this sentence: "If I had _____ , I wouldn't wish for anything else."

2. **Set** – Philippians 4:10-13 – Why is it hard to be content when we are "well fed" and "living in plenty"?

3. **Go** – How does a person get the strength that Jesus offers? What makes it hard for you to trust him?

Chapter 5 – We are intentionally designed by God.

1. **Ready** – If you know (or can look it up), tell us the meaning of your name.

2. **Set** – Ephesians 2:10 – If you are God's craft project, how do you feel about his style? What would you have done differently?

3. **Go** – Tell us something you really like about yourself.

Chapter 6 – Anyone can lead—by example.

1. **Ready** – Do you like to lead, or do you prefer to follow? When and where?

2. **Set** – 1 Timothy 4:12 – Who is a good example to you in the way they talk? Or the way they live? Or their love? Or their faith? Or their reliability?

3. **Go** – Think of someone (but don't tell us) who treats you like a little kid. How could you be an example to them?

Chapter 7 – God guides us with our minds.

1. **Ready** – Do you usually ask for directions, or do you prefer to find your way on your own? Any stories about getting lost?

2. **Set** – Psalm 32:8-9 – What are the ways God says he will guide you? How should people be different from animals?

3. **Go** – Tell us about a current situation where you don't know what to do.

Chapter 8 – We are the sheep and Jesus is the Shepherd (not the other way around).

1. **Ready** – Tell us everything you know about sheep! Did you know they can recognize up to 50 other sheep faces and remember them for two years?

2. **Set** – Isaiah 53: 6-7 – This is a prophecy about Jesus. How are we like sheep? How did Jesus the Shepherd save us?

3. **Go** – What do you think about Jesus? Baaaa, humbug? Or are you ready to follow him as your Shepherd?

Chapter 9 – God takes nobodies and turns them into somebodies.

1. **Ready** – Who have you met that is famous? How famous are you?

2. **Set** – 1 Corinthians 1:26-29 – Why do you think God is so interested in ordinary people?

3. **Go** – What's your story? Would anyone like to tell us about your life so far?

Chapter 10 – A lifetime of trusting God will help you in scary situations.

1. **Ready** – Tell us about a time when you were afraid and didn't know how things would turn out.

2. **Set** – Psalm 56:3-4 – Do you think you will trust God when you run into trouble if you haven't trusted God before that time?

3. **Go** – Tell God—with one word—what makes you afraid.

Chapter 11 – Our own resources are limited, but God's are not.

1. **Ready** – What are you really good at doing? Who is better at doing that thing than you?

2. **Set** – Jeremiah 17:5-8 (or just 7-8) – Are you a person who depends on God, or would you rather depend on yourself? What are your reasons?

3. **Go** – *Cabin leader: Tell a story about a time when you were at the end of your rope and needed to trust God.*

Chapter 12 – Jesus is the Way.

1. **Ready** – *Take a look at a compass (on your phone, if needed).* Does anyone know how a compass works? *(Look up "compass" at kids.britannica.com)*

2. **Set** – John 14:6 – People who seek "the Way" are people who know they are lost. Do you feel like you need Jesus to be "the Way" for you?

3. **Go** – Is today the day for you to believe in Jesus, the Way, the Truth and the Life?

Chapter 13 – God invites us to ask him boldly.

1. **Ready** – Tell us about a time you asked God for something you really wanted.

2. **Set** – Luke 11:5-10 – Why does Jesus want us to be bold when we ask for something?

3. **Go** – What will you dare to ask God for? Do you think he will say yes or no?

Chapter 14 – With Jesus, there are no ordinary days.

1. **Ready** – Have you ever had an extraordinary day? Tell us about it.

2. **Set** – John 10:1-14, especially verse 10. What do you like about the way Jesus talks about his sheep?

3. **Go** – Jesus offers you a full, abundant life. How does it become yours?

Chapter 15 – Knowing the truth about Jesus sets people free.

1. **Ready** – Who do you know that is in need of a compass right now?

2. **Set** – John 8:31-32. What kinds of things take people captive? How would knowing the truth set them free?

3. **Go** – What are you going to tell your friends and family back home about your week at camp?

Also by Jim Badke, for leaders:

The Christian Camp Leader

Will you serve at a
Christian camp this
summer? Then this
book is for you!
Prepare your heart,
focus your perspective
and hone your skills as
a camp leader.

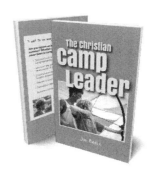

*"The Christian Camp Leader is well-written, accessible
and concise, showing rookies—and reminding veterans—
what camp ministry is all about."* – Bill McCaskell,
One Hope Canada

Jim Badke writes from 40+
years of church and camp
ministry. He and his wife
Sarah and their dog Barkley
live by the lake in
Honeymoon Bay on
Vancouver Island.

---Available on Amazon---
ISBN 978-0-9916846-2-5

Also by Jim Badke, for leaders:

As The Eagle Walks

If the Apostle John was still living on the island of Patmos, would you want to visit him?

Touring the Mediterranean to save a crumbling marriage, Jason explores the island of Patmos and meets a man who claims to be the Apostle John. Invited to stay with him for a while, Jason wrestles with the gap he sees between John and his own understanding of Christian faith. Some Islanders love this man and others hate him. Will Jason uncover why?

"As The Eagle Walks *pulled me in from its first page and held me with its richly-drawn characters, vividly-evoked scenes, crisp and often funny dialogue, and mounting tension—all the things we look for in a novel—while exploring real-life matters of faith.*"

– Mark Buchanan, author of *God Walk* and *David Rise*

---Available on Amazon---
ISBN 978-1777710101

Manufactured by Amazon.ca
Bolton, ON